Takers and Returners

Carol Beach York, who was born in Chicago, is a full-time
writer with many outstanding books for children to her credit.
Several of her stories for younger children have been
published in England as well as the United States. She now
lives with her daughter in a big old house in Harvey, Illinois.

Carol Beach York

Takers and Returners

Piccolo Pan Books
in association with Heinemann

First published in Great Britain 1974 by William Heinemann Ltd
This edition published 1979 by Pan Books Ltd,
Cavaye Place, London SW10 9PG
in association with William Heinemann Ltd
© Carol Beach York 1973
ISBN 0 330 25812 5
Printed in Great Britain by
Richard Clay (The Chaucer Press) Ltd, Bungay, Suffolk

for my daughter Diana
whose pastimes are most innocent

Contents

'I've thought of a game,' said my cousin Julian.

We were all sitting around the hammock at the back of our yard, shielded from sight from the house by a row of lilac bushes, their leaves gone dusty in the dry days of late July. Kitty and I in the hammock, the three boys stretched out on the grass, and Jenny playing with a doll under the lilac bushes.

'Who wants to play a dull old game?' Kitty muttered.

But I was intrigued. 'What kind of a game?' I asked.

'A different kind of game,' Julian said. 'We've never played it before.'

In the still, sunlit afternoon there was no hint, no forewarning of danger. Cam propped himself up on the grass, and Andy eased his face out from under the baseball cap.

'What's it called?' Cam asked.

Julian thought a moment. Then he smiled slowly. 'We'll call it Takers and Returners.'

the Carter children
Ellen, age thirteen
Kitty, age twelve
Cameron (Cam), age fourteen

their cousins
Julian, age fifteen
Jenny, age seven

their friend
Andy Foster, age twelve

1 Choosing sides

Our summers at Green Hill Lake had always been happy times. But then came the summer I was thirteen. And I guess that's an unlucky number, like breaking a mirror or having a black cat cross your path – no, that's silly, I don't really believe in things like that.

But that summer *was* different.

It even began wrong. In little ways that didn't mean much by themselves. The sink drain didn't run right when we arrived, and we had a lot of trouble before we got it fixed. Then Mother heard that the Martin family wasn't coming that summer, and she was sorry because they were good friends of hers and she looked forward to seeing them at Green Hill.

I didn't mind much about the drain or that the Martins weren't coming. They didn't have any children we played with anyway. Our cousins Julian and Jenny were always at Green Hill for the summer (Father and Uncle Peter came out for weekends), in a house down the road from ours, and we ran back and forth along a special not-for-grown-ups trail we had discovered across backyards and between hedges, where dark emerald shadows lay across the grass, and we could hear bees humming.

At first it was like all the other summers since we had been coming to Green Hill. My sister Kitty and I slept late, and Father called us his sleeping beauties. We went swimming and rowing, and walked into the village to the movies. All the things we had always done. Nothing was different or seemed likely to be so.

Andy Foster, who lived at the lake all year round, hung around with us, as he always had, pedalling over on a bicycle prone to flat tyres and other ailments.

('Here comes Tubby,' Cam used to say, until Mother overheard him one day and told him to stop.)

Dr Drover waved to us when he drove by, his kindly face unchanged by the years.

And Miss Mindy was there in her yellow house, wearing gloves to prune her rose bushes in the warm green afternoons.

Nothing had changed.

My brother Cam, money-hungry as usual, took the summer job of mowing Miss Mindy's lawn.

'Boy, that's money-hungry,' Kitty marvelled.

Miss Mindy was a stern old lady with a snappish little grey dog named Sammy, and she was pretty fussy about things. Kitty said she probably measured the blades of grass when Cam mowed, to see that he had them all even. But he got his money. About midsummer Miss Mindy went away to visit her sister, leaving Cam in charge of her yard and her next-door neighbours in charge of Sammy.

I always loved getting to Green Hill when school was out and summer vacation began.

But my sister Kitty hadn't wanted to come this summer.

'I wish we'd go some place else some summer for a change,' she complained the very first day as we were unpacking our clothes in our room. She was a year younger than I, and inclined by nature to be restless and discontent with the sameness of things. In the city, during school time, she complained about school: 'I wish I could go away to school and not come to this old place every day of my life.' Or she would say she wished she could quit school and start her *life*. She was head of her class at school, so I don't know why she complained about it so much. If Cam and I could only sail through maths and things with Kitty's ease!

Kitty had always found plenty of things to do at Green Hill in summers before, but right away that summer – that summer I was thirteen and Kitty was twelve – she began to get bored. Sometimes the rest of us would leave her sitting moodily in the hammock while we went down to the lake. 'That old lake,' she would say with a sigh: 'Who wants to go there every day?'

By mid-July she was just about ready for any change from the sameness of Green Hill.

My cousin Julian was fifteen that summer, the oldest of us and the one whose lead we all seemed to follow. He had always been a handsome boy, with dark hair and eyes, and before I found out you couldn't marry a cousin, I had always thought I would like to grow up and marry Julian.

'Cousins don't marry, Ellen,' Mother had explained to me when I was about ten. 'At least not first cousins.'

'They don't?'

I must have looked crestfallen, for my father said, 'Cheer up, sweetie, there're a lot of fish in the ocean.'

'But I wanted to marry Julian.'

My father just laughed, but my mother had a withdrawn look on her face that puzzled me.

'You don't like Julian,' I accused her.

She turned away and got busy putting some silverware in a kitchen drawer. 'Don't be silly, Ellen,' she said.

But I was heartbroken for a while that cousins couldn't marry. And I thought maybe we would marry anyway and that Mother really did like Julian. She was always just as nice to him as she was to everybody else. The only criticism she made about their family was that her sister Lily – who was Julian's and Jenny's mother – was spoiling Jenny and that what the child needed was discipline.

Jenny was quite a bit younger than the rest of us. She

was only seven the summer I was thirteen. She was dark-haired like Julian, and she was skinny. That was because she was picky with her food, Mother said. And Jenny was a whiner if she didn't get her way about things. But she had grown up tagging around after us older kids at Green Hill, and we were used to having her with us.

The day Julian told us about the game had been a hot day. A laziness brought on by the heat and the hum of cicadas high in the treetops had lulled us all. Even Jenny squatting with her doll in the shade of the lilac bush had ceased to play and sat absently, not even listening to us, twisting a strand of hair in her fingers – a habit she had picked up that summer and which was driving her mother, and my mother, wild.

'It's worse than the summer she sucked her fingers,' my Aunt Lily said. To which my mother replied, 'Well, maybe. Neither is nice.'

On that hot day, we were all as bored as Kitty. Even swimming and fishing in the lake didn't seem interesting, and we had already seen the movie at the only theatre in Green Hill Village.

Time seemed to have nothing to offer us but the heat and the bright sun and the sound of the cicadas we could only hear but never see. Their drone rose and fell, building to a loud shriek and then cutting off abruptly into silence.

'I've thought of a game,' said my cousin Julian.

'Who wants to play a dull old game?' Kitty muttered.

But I was intrigued. 'What kind of a game?' I asked.

'A different kind of game,' Julian said. 'We've never played it before.'

In the still, sunlit afternoon, there was no hint, no forewarning of danger. Cam propped himself up on the grass, and Andy eased his face out from under the baseball cap.

14

'What's it called?' Cam asked.

Julian thought a moment. Then he smiled slowly. 'We'll call it Takers and Returners.'

'We have to choose up sides for this game,' Julian went on.

'Can I be captain of one side?' Kitty wanted to know right away.

'I'll be a captain,' Julian said, 'because I thought of the game. We'll draw names for the other one.'

Kitty looked disgruntled. 'I never win when we draw names,' she objected. 'And I don't see why you get to be a captain just because you thought of the game.'

'I won't tell you what it is then.'

Kitty glared at him darkly a moment and then gave in. 'All right for you. Be an old captain.'

Julian began to write something on a pad of paper he had taken from his pocket. When he tore the paper into four strips, each strip had a name written on it. He hadn't made a slip for himself, because he was already going to be a captain, or one for Jenny because she was too little.

We all watched solemnly as Julian folded the four pieces of paper into tight squares.

'Here.' I offered him the straw hat Mother always wanted me to wear because my skin was fair and I sunburned easily – and that I took off as soon as I was out of sight of the house.

Julian turned the hat upside down and put the papers in.

'You draw,' he said, thrusting the hat towards Cam, who was lying closest to him on the grass.

Kitty crossed her fingers that she would be chosen, and Cam made a great to-do about reaching into the hat. He pushed back imaginary cuffs and rubbed his hands together like a magician about to pull out a rabbit. Andy snickered with admiration at these dramatics.

When Cam had at last extracted one of the slips from the hat, he made a pretence of surprise and clutched it to his chest so that no one else could see it.

'Honestly!' Kitty snatched the paper away from him with exasperation. It was almost torn in two, but she could read it well enough. 'Ellen,' she announced with a deflated sigh. 'See, I told you. I never win.'

Julian nodded with satisfaction – whether because he was glad Kitty had lost or I had won, I couldn't tell.

'Now do we choose up sides?' Andy asked.

'You can choose first, Ellen,' Julian said, looking at me intently.

Something in his expression made me uneasy. Somehow I felt whoever I chose, it would be wrong. Julian was the only one who knew what the game was going to be. How could I know who to choose when I didn't know what we were choosing for?

'Tell us the game first,' I said.

He shook his head, and his dark eyes closed mysteriously. 'No. You choose first. We have to choose first and then I'll tell.'

'Go ahead, Ellen. Don't take all day,' Cam said.

That wasn't fair, I thought. If we were going to play running games, I should choose Kitty because she was the fastest runner.

Cam poked at my shoe with his foot. 'Go *on*.'

I looked around thoughtfully. If I chose Cam, it wouldn't be really fun, because Cam and Julian liked to do everything together, and maybe Cam wouldn't even play then. But I thought I ought to have at least one boy on my team.

'I choose Andy,' I said.

Right away I felt guilty at how his round, freckled face lighted up under the thatch of sun-bleached hair. Andy was not good at games usually, being too short-legged and stocky, and he never got picked first on teams. He and

Jenny were always the leftovers when we had to take sides for anything.

If Julian was surprised at my choice, he didn't let on. But what *he* did surprised me even more.

'I choose Jenny,' he said.

Jenny! What good could she be? Nobody ever chose her until she was the only one left to choose.

But Julian never did things without a good reason.

'I think you ought to tell us what the game is,' I said again. 'How can I choose when I don't know what it's for?'

'Oh, for Pete's sake.' Cam rolled over and covered his head with his arms.

'Go on, Ellen,' Julian directed calmly.

I stared back at him, trying to read something in his face, some clue, something – which of course was impossible.

'All right,' I said at last, 'I choose Kitty.'

That left Cam to be on Julian's team.

'Now tell us what the game is,' Kitty said eagerly. She was over her crossness about not being captain. 'Whatever it is, I bet Ellen and Andy and I can beat you and Cam.'

'But can you beat Jenny?' Julian said mockingly.

Then he began to laugh, because Kitty threw a pillow off the hammock at him and missed by a mile.

I hoped it wasn't a game of throwing skills, with Kitty on my side.

Jenny came out from under the lilac bushes, dragging her doll by a leg. It looked forlorn bumping along the grass, face down and pulled by its leg. She dragged it a little way and then left it there, abandoned in the grass.

2 Rules of the game

'It's a simple game really,' Julian said.

He watched as Jenny ran away, chasing a butterfly.

'It's a test of wits, among ourselves. And also a test of our brains against the grown-ups.'

Cam snorted. He sunburned easily too, just as I did, and his nose was peeling. I thought he looked very funny.

'What is it?' Kitty persisted. Her dark eyes glowed with anticipation.

'Before I tell you,' Julian said, 'you have to promise not ever to tell. Not before we start or during the game or afterwards when it's over. Nobody ever tells.'

'All right,' we all promised solemnly.

'It's really simple,' Julian repeated. 'Each team takes something here in Green Hill – something the grown-ups will miss and start looking for—'

'You mean stealing?' Kitty interrupted with surprise.

'Let me finish.' Julian held up his hand. 'No, not stealing. We're going to return the things. It's a test of wits, I told you. Each team takes something, and then the other team has to return it without getting caught by the grown-ups.'

We were all silent a moment, and then Cam said, 'But that's dumb. I could take that bronze bird my dad has on his desk and hand it to Kitty or Ellen or Andy, and they could set it back on the desk.'

Julian looked at Cam with weary patience. 'Very funny,' he said.

'Be quiet, Cam, and let Julian explain,' Kitty commanded.

'There are rules, of course.' Julian glanced at Cam. 'One of the rules is that whatever is taken has to be taken *away*.

And it has to be something they'll really be looking for. If they find it, that team loses. The other team has to get it back without being caught, or they lose.'

We were all silent again. Even Kitty. Her mind was probably racing, but she didn't say a word.

'For instance,' Julian said, 'my team could take something like that bronze bird Cam mentioned. His dad has had that for years. He'd really start a big hunt if it was suddenly missing.'

'He'd probably call in the police,' Cam said, half joking.

'Anyway,' Julian continued, 'we could take it and hide it – or, bury it in the woods or something like that. Your dad would be looking everywhere for it. Maybe they would question us. Maybe they *would* call the police and report a burglary.'

Kitty shivered. That wasn't like Kitty. But something – I don't know – made me feel shivery too.

'Then the other team would have to get into the woods and dig it up and somehow get it back into the house and on the desk without being seen. Like in the middle of the night maybe.'

'Hey, right on!' Cam said.

'Yeah, right on!' Andy echoed. But he didn't sound quite as enthused as Cam. I didn't think he'd really like the idea of sneaking into our house in the middle of the night.

I hugged my arms closer around me and stared at Julian. It was the strangest game I had ever heard of.

Julian leaned back and smiled. He was sure we would all go along with him. We always had.

'What do you say, Ellen?' Kitty demanded, watching me hopefully.

'I don't think so.'

'Aw – come on, Ellen. It would be something to *do*.'

'Ellen's afraid,' Julian said tauntingly.

'It's not that—'

But of course it was. At least partly. How awful to get caught! But that wasn't the only thing. Somehow it didn't seem right, the whole idea.

Everybody was waiting for me to decide. I looked at Andy. I was sure he really wouldn't want to play a game like that either. But I knew it would be useless to wait for him to speak up and take my side. Andy never made decisions.

'You're spoiling everything.' Kitty pouted.

And then from the house I heard Mother calling us. 'Give me my hat,' I said.

Cam handed it to me, and the three other pieces of paper that had been in the drawing tumbled out on the grass.

'Come on, Kitty,' I said. 'Mother's calling.'

'Think about it, Ellen,' Julian called after us.

But I didn't answer.

3 The game begins

I thought that would be the end of it, but I should have known better. Julian didn't like to be put down – and I had run away without even a backward look.

He came over that night after supper and stood by the side of the front yard where Kitty and I had put up the croquet set. 'For lack of anything better to do,' Kitty had said pointedly, meaning that if I had agreed to try Julian's game, we would have something better to do than play croquet with paint-chipped balls and two wickets missing.

'Have you thought about what we were talking about this afternoon?' Julian wanted to know.

'No, I haven't.' I frowned and tried to concentrate on my next shot.

'I thought you were a better sport than that.'

'It's a silly game,' I said. 'It wouldn't work.'

I aimed at the next wicket and missed.

'Think about it some more,' Julian said. He sauntered off towards the house, and a little while later he and Cam came back out past our croquet game and walked off in the direction of the village.

'Where're you going?' Kitty called after them. I suppose she thought anything would be better than croquet.

Cam looked back mischievously. He didn't answer at once, and then a big grin broke across his silly, sunburned face. 'To the library.'

'Ha ha,' Kitty retorted.

Wild horses couldn't drag Cam into the library during summer vacation. Cam's grin almost broke his face. Wherever they *were* going, he sure thought it was funny.

We watched as Cam and Julian walked away down the road.

'I wonder where they're really going,' Kitty said.

Where they were really going, we soon found out, was to the library.

The first thing I saw when I opened my eyes the next morning was a twelve-inch-high bust of Charles Dickens sitting on the bureau.

At first I didn't know it was Dickens, of course. I looked at it curiously, sleepily – and then I realized that I wasn't asleep. I was awake. And there was a statue on my bureau where there hadn't been a statue the night before.

I stood by the bureau and read the gold lettering at the bottom of the bust. 'CHARLES DICKENS 1812–1870.' What on earth ... ?

'What's *that*?' Kitty had wakened and was sitting up in bed rubbing her eyes.

'I don't know.'

I lifted the statue curiously and found a slip of folded paper lying underneath.

As I unfolded the paper, Kitty came to stand beside me, reading over my shoulder.

This item has been missing from the Green Hill Library since last night. Miss Adams will be very happy to have it safely returned.

'Julian and Cam,' Kitty exclaimed. 'They took it, Ellen – and now we've got to return it!'

'No, we don't. We'll just give it right back to them.'

'You don't want them to think we can't do it!' Kitty protested. She stood there in her shortie pyjamas, her hair tousled, her face flushed with excitement. 'And we *can* do it, Ellen. If they got it out, we can get it back in.'

'Kitty—'

'What's the harm?' she insisted. 'Just tell me what's the harm. Miss Adams probably hasn't even missed it yet. We can go right down this morning and get it back before she does. That ought to show Cam and Julian we're as smart as they are.'

I stood staring at the bust. Cam (I was sure it was Cam – he always thought of goofy things) had drawn curly pencil marks on the moustache.

'And if Miss Adams *has* missed it, think how happy she'll be to have it returned! It will be a good deed! We can smuggle it in – oh, Ellen, it will be exciting.'

'How could we smuggle it in?' I objected. The statue was much too big to be hidden under the skimpy blouses and shorts we wore.

'We can get some bags, and it will look like we've been shopping,' Kitty planned rapidly. 'Then we can go behind some shelves and unpack.'

I could hear paper bags crackling loudly in the silence of the library while we 'unpacked'. But I also began to have twinges of a feeling of challenge. Maybe just this one time, just to show Julian ...

'A bag wouldn't do at all. A paper bag would be too noisy.'

Kitty shrugged this off easily. 'Okay, we'll think of something else.'

'Maybe that nylon shopping bag Mom has ...' I rubbed at the pencil marks. Whatever we did, I wasn't going to return CHARLES DICKENS 1812–1870 with a pencilled moustache.

'Won't they be surprised, Ellen. I bet they think we won't have the nerve to do it.'

I began to feel excited myself. If Cam and Julian could get Charles Dickens out of the library under Miss Adams' beady-eyed scrutiny, Kitty and I could get him back. Kitty and I and Andy, I reminded myself. Andy was part of my team too.

But as it turned out, we had to go without Andy. We put the bust into the nylon shopping bag – which was easy enough to borrow from the kitchen drawer where Mother always kept it. We put one of Kitty's sweaters in on top, so nobody could see what was in the bag. Then we went to Andy's house to show him the statue and the note we had found. But his mother said he had gone out riding on his bike.

'I wonder where he's riding,' I said to Kitty as we walked back to the road from Andy's house.

'We'll never find him. Let's go without him. We can tell him about it later.'

'Maybe we'll meet him on the way,' I said. 'Maybe he just rode into the village, and we'll meet him coming back.'

But we didn't. We got all the way into the village and to the foot of the library steps without seeing Andy and his bicycle.

At the foot of the library steps we stopped. I sat down on the bottom step, the bag between my knees, and stared down at the top of it where Kitty's red sweater was trailing out by one arm.

'What are you waiting for?' Kitty cried, hovering restlessly over me.

'We can't go in the way you look.' Her eyes were about to pop with excitement. 'Try to calm down and look normal. And tuck your blouse in.'

Kitty made a gesture at tucking in her blouse.

'Now try not to look so excited,' I cautioned. I got up and took a sturdy grip on the handles of the bag. I hoped the bag wouldn't break halfway across the library floor. What a smack that would make in that still, still room. And

CHARLES DICKENS 1812–1870 – well, that would be the end of him altogether.

'Do I look calm?' Kitty still looked suspiciously bright-eyed to me, but I guess it was the best she could do.

'Try to keep your face down and maybe Miss Adams won't notice.'

My hands felt clammy on the handles, and the bag bumped uncomfortably against my legs.

But up the stairs we went.

Into the library.

We were as brave and smart as Julian and Cam. And we were going to prove it to them.

4 The next move?

The library was as silent as a tomb. Miss Adams glanced up as we came in and smiled her usual rather tight-lipped smile. I always felt that she didn't actually like people coming into the library, disturbing the silence with footsteps and whispering, disturbing the careful order of the books upon the shelves.

Our footsteps echoed on the polished floor as Kitty and I marched past the desk with our bumpy bag and got ourselves out of sight behind a stretch of books in the history section.

On each low window sill around the library a plaster bust of a writer had been set – although the only one I had ever recognized was Shakespeare. I left Kitty to guard the bag and made a foray from behind the history shelves to see if I could spot an empty window sill – and, sure enough, there was one, looking bare and bleak.

Mercifully it was near the back of the library. If Miss Adams did not turn her head at the wrong moment – I crossed my fingers and edged back between the stacks to Kitty.

'It's that last window over there,' I whispered.

'Can I do it?' Kitty was trembling with eagerness.

She bent down and began to push aside the sweater that covered the statue.

I hesitated. I was captain, maybe I should do it – but Kitty already had the statue out of the bag.

'Please, Ellen – I know I can do it.'

'All right. Keep the sweater around it until you get to the window, and be sure she's not looking before you put it back.'

Kitty nodded, bright-eyed and flushed.

'And, Kitty, *don't drop it.*'

I lurked behind the bookshelves, peeking alternately at Miss Adams at the front desk and Kitty tiptoeing towards the window. At the window Kitty paused and looked furtively over her shoulder. Miss Adams' head was bent down. She did not turn. Kitty fumbled amid the folds of the sweater, and, presto chango – there was CHARLES DICKENS 1812–1870 back in his spot again.

After that we got out of the library as fast as we could. We didn't want to be there if Miss Adams suddenly decided to get up and walk around and discovered that the statue was back. (If she had noticed it was missing.) On that quiet July morning there was not another soul in the library, and Miss Adams would certainly have put two and two together.

On our way home, now that all was over and done, we finally met Andy. He was pumping his bicycle uphill, red-faced and perspiring, his baseball cap askew on his head.

Breathless with victory, Kitty told him what 'our team' had just done, and he listened with an expression of growing admiration for our daring. 'Hey, you really *did* that? Boy, would I like to see Miss Adams' face when she turns around, and there's that old statue right back in place.'

My heart had pounded every echoing step of the way across the library room. But it was over now. We had done it. And looking back, it didn't seem so awfully hard after all. In fact, it had been fun, sort of, sneaking that statue back into its place, right under Miss Adams' nose. Exciting. It made me tingle to remember it.

'It was easy,' I said, with the tone of someone who returned statues to libraries every day of the week.

'Like a ghost had been there or something.' Kitty bubbled with exhilaration. 'One day it disappears, the next day it appears again. Now *we've* got to take something for Julian and Cam and Jenny to return, don't we, Ellen?' She tugged at my arm urgently.

I frowned down at the stubble of grass growing along the path. Maybe – we could just this once.

We continued our way homeward with Andy pedalling slowly beside us, discarding first one idea then another. At Miss Mindy's house the grass looked as if it could use a cutting, but Cam was nowhere in sight.

'Let's see if he's around back,' Kitty suggested. 'I can't wait to tell him we got the statue back to the library.'

We walked across the lawn and around the side of the house, but the back yard was deserted. In the yard next door Miss Mindy's dog Sammy came barking fiercely at the fence. I didn't envy the Lang family their dog-sitting job.

'Hi there, Sammy.' Andy went up to the fence and undid the gate, but Kitty and I hung back. Andy was one of the few people Sammy didn't snap at, and Kitty and I never went any nearer to Sammy than we could help.

Sammy's barking stopped, and he let Andy rub the back of his head. 'How've you been?' Andy said to him. He whined and pawed at Andy's knee.

'Come on, Andy,' Kitty called impatiently. 'We've got things to do.'

Andy came back, carefully locking the Langs' gate so Sammy couldn't get out.

'Hey,' he said. 'There's a pie cooling on Mrs Lang's back window sill. How about taking that?'

I couldn't help laughing. 'Andy – a *pie*?'

'Nobody's around.' He pushed back the baseball cap and rubbed the crease it had made on his forehead.

'We couldn't do that,' I said. 'That would be a dirty trick. It's probably for their supper tonight.'

'But wouldn't that be funny?' Kitty giggled. 'Think

how silly Cam and Julian would look taking back a pie.'

'No,' I said firmly. 'Nobody's pies.'

We started on our way again, and Kitty and Andy kept laughing about how funny it would be to take Mrs Lang's pie.

Our steps began to lag, however, as we got closer and closer to Aunt Lily's house. We could see Julian and Cam sitting on the porch rail, and we wanted to tell them what we'd done. But we hadn't thought of anything to take yet ourselves.

'We've got to think of *something*,' Kitty said frantically.

Andy lolled on his bike, digging his shoes into the grass. After his suggestion about Mrs Lang's pie, I didn't expect much help from him.

'I know, I know,' Kitty whispered suddenly. She pulled me around to face her and continued urgently, 'Now *don't* look up at the *roof*, *don't* look up at the *roof*.'

'For Pete's sake, Kitty—'

But she rushed on. 'Andy, listen, listen—' She caught his arm excitedly. 'We can take the weathervane!'

Andy's eyes automatically went to the house and up to the roof.

'*Don't look at the roof*. You'll give it all away! Julian's watching us this very minute.'

Andy and I tried to look every place but at Aunt Lily's roof.

'And I know just how we can do it,' Kitty went on rapidly. 'Tonight we're all going to The Cedars for dinner – remember, Ellen?' I nodded vaguely, and for Andy's information Kitty explained, 'Our family is going with Julian's family – nobody will be here tonight.'

She paused to let the words sink in, and as Andy did not look very enlightened, she repeated meaningfully, 'Nobody will be here at this house tonight, for at least two or three hours anyway.'

Andy stared back at Kitty blankly.

'All you have to do is get a ladder and get up on the roof and take down the weathervane!'

Andy's mouth opened, but he didn't say anything. I wouldn't go up more than two steps on a ladder, but I didn't know how Andy felt about them.

'You wouldn't be afraid, would you?' Kitty urged brightly. 'It's not a very high roof.'

Andy's eyes went back to measure the height of the roof and Kitty groaned. 'Don't look at the house, stupid! You'll give it away.'

Andy stared down at his bicycle handle.

'You could do it, couldn't you, Andy?' She shook his arm.

'Gee, I don't know ...'

'Ellen and I had to go to the library. It's your turn to do something for the team.'

'But Kitty—' I began, but she cut me off.

'Andy can do it, Ellen. He isn't afraid of ladders, are you, Andy?'

'No,' Andy said uncertainly. He looked at the house again. No doubt the roof looked much higher to him, who would have to get a ladder and go up on it, than it looked to Kitty, who would be at The Cedars eating dinner.

'It's settled then,' Kitty said triumphantly. 'That ought to surprise Julian and Cam. It's a lot more daring than taking a silly old statue off a window sill three feet high.'

'Yeah, it sure is,' Andy agreed to that willingly enough. He began to look more enthused.

Before I could protest further, Kitty left us and set off across the front lawn towards the porch.

I lingered behind with Andy for a moment. 'Can you do it, Andy?'

'Sure,' he said boldly. 'Sure, I can.'

All I could think, as we followed Kitty towards the

30

porch, was, What if he breaks a leg or something? Andy was usually so clumsy. And again misgivings about the whole game flooded over me.

By the time we reached the porch, Kitty had already told Julian and Cam about going to the library.

'You really did it!' Cam punched her arm playfully. 'I didn't think you had the nerve.'

'It was easy. We're just as smart as you two any old day. Wait till you see what we take.'

Julian was listening with interest.

Oh, Andy, I thought helplessly, don't stick your foot through the roof. Don't fall off the ladder. Don't fall off that roof. I didn't think I was going to be able to eat much at The Cedars, worrying about Andy and the ladder and the roof shingles and the weathervane.

I began to wish we'd taken Mrs Lang's pie. She could have made Jell-o or something for dessert. But it was too late now.

5 Ellen's team

That evening our family and Julian's family all drove to
The Cedars for dinner. We usually did this once or twice
during a summer.

The Cedars had been converted from a large old
private residence to a restaurant. The oak floors gleamed
with polish, and in the main dining room three leaded
bay windows overlooked a garden sloping down to a
pond strewn with lily pads. A short distance behind the
house, a servants' quarters had been made into a gift shop.
Mother and Aunt Lily liked to poke around in the shop
after dinner while the men sat in the garden.

All the way on the drive to The Cedars, Kitty kept
whispering to me, 'Won't Aunt Lily and Uncle Peter be
surprised when they get home!'

My main concern was still for Andy Foster getting up
and down that ladder safely. All through dinner I thought
of him, pudgy and puffing, crouched on the roof. I could
hardly even eat.

After dinner Kitty and I went along with Mother and
Aunt Lily to the gift shop. Jenny came too, and the
browsing was punctuated by Aunt Lily's frequent appeals
to Jenny:

'Don't touch that, dear.'

'Don't pick up the china.'

'Just *look*, or we'll have to leave.'

Mother bought a wall plaque of sunflowers carved in
wood, and Aunt Lily bought a long string of blue crystal
beads. She bought some imported hard candies in a tiny
green-and-gold tin box for Jenny. Jenny spilled most of

them on the grass as we walked back to the garden, and Aunt Lily's admonitions began again:

'Jenny, you should be more careful, dear ... now why didn't you let Mama open the box for you?'

But Kitty and I had other things on our minds. It was time to head for home, and we exchanged eloquent glances as we got into the car. Cam rode with Julian in Uncle Peter's car, late-evening sunlight glinting on the chrome as it turned out of The Cedars' parking area and started along the road back to Green Hill. Our car followed close behind. Jenny had begged to ride with us, and she fell asleep between Kitty and me in the back seat, looking angelic, her empty tin box in her lap, wisps of dark hair blowing softly across her cheeks.

The arrival at Julian's house was all Kitty could have hoped for. Aunt Lily was already out of the car ahead, staring with considerable surprise at the roof of her house. To my relief there was no sign of Andy lying on the ground, unconscious or broken-legged.

As our car came to a stop in the drive behind Uncle Peter's car, Aunt Lily turned and called to Mother.

'Look at this, Marian. Our weathervane's gone!'

6 Keeping score

Even Julian and Cam had to admit it was a more daring feat than CHARLES DICKENS 1812–1870.

Single-handed, Andy had lugged the heavy weathervane down the ladder and hidden it in a bush-shrouded nook at the far end of Aunt Lily's back yard.

'You're wonderful!' Kitty almost hugged Andy when we met him the next day.

Andy beamed foolishly. 'Oh, sure.'

All afternoon we hung around Aunt Lily's house, waiting to see what Julian and Cam would do. There wasn't much they *could* do, actually, with Aunt Lily and Uncle Peter home. They said they were going swimming, and then hid at the back of the yard by the weathervane-bushes to see if Aunt Lily and Uncle Peter would go away somewhere.

But it didn't look as if Aunt Lily and Uncle Peter were going anywhere.

Kitty and Andy and I ranged ourselves on the porch steps and ate green grapes and enjoyed Julian and Cam's dilemma.

'If Aunt Lily and Uncle Peter don't go out somewhere for a while, Cam and Julian will have to climb up and put the weathervane back in the dead of night,' Kitty said with a delighted shiver.

I looked at her uneasily. 'That sounds pretty risky to me.'

'It was hard enough in daylight,' Andy agreed.

Kitty was undauntable. 'But wouldn't that be exciting?'

Jenny was squatting in the front yard, digging a hole in the lawn with a bent spoon. 'I'm planting a flower,' she called to us.

By and by she came and sat on the steps with us and picked at the grape stems with tiny grubby fingers. 'How soon will my flower grow?' she asked me hopefully.

'It will probably take a few days,' I answered vaguely. 'What did you plant?'

'A seed.'

She was silent a moment. 'If I plant a grape, will it grow?'

'Why don't you try it and see?' Kitty suggested dreamily. I could tell she was still lost in her thoughts of Cam and Julian on the rooftop in 'the dead of night'.

Jenny took a grape and ran back to the grass to find her spoon. The sun had reached the end of the yard, and deep pools of shade lay about the trees. The afternoon seemed endless.

Finally, about four o'clock, Aunt Lily came out on the porch and called Jenny in to wash her face and hands. 'Daddy and I are going into the village,' Aunt Lily said, 'and you can't go with those dirty hands.'

Kitty and Andy and I scattered like dandelion puffs. We didn't want to be known to have been anywhere near the house when the weathervane miraculously reappeared – as we were sure it would as soon as Aunt Lily and Uncle Peter and Jenny went to the village.

Of course that meant we missed the fun of seeing Julian and Cam going up the ladder and hammering the cumbersome old weathercock back into place. But we did have the satisfaction of a visit from Aunt Lily shortly after supper-time that night. She came bustling along the hallway to the kitchen, where Kitty and I were helping Mother with the supper dishes.

'You'll never guess what,' Aunt Lily announced. Her gentle grey eyes sparkled as she anticipated the surprise she was going to give us.

'What?' Mother wiped her hands on her apron as she turned from the sink.

'The weathervane's back.'

'It is?' Mother said with amazement.

'It is?' Kitty and I echoed innocently.

'Yes, it is.'

'But who—?' Mother began, and Aunt Lily shook her head at the puzzle of it all. 'Nobody knows. We were all gone. Julian was swimming with Cam, nobody was home. I guess we'll never know how it got back.'

'But why would anybody even take it in the first place?' Mother murmured. 'Now isn't that a mystery?'

Kitty and I wiped solemnly at our silverware and dinner plates.

We had played the game. And it had worked.

Late the next afternoon Kitty and I were reading in the hammock by the lilac bushes when Cam and Julian and Andy came along. It was unbearably hot, with a brilliant blue sky above, scattered with puffy white clouds.

Julian sat down on the grass, leaning back against one of the trees that supported the hammock. 'I've been thinking we ought to keep score some way,' he said.

I raised up in the hammock and twisted around to look at him.

'Score for what?'

'For the game.'

'But we've played the game. You don't think up scores after the game is over.'

Cam and Andy sprawled beside Julian. 'You don't want to stop now, do you?' Cam said. 'This is fun.' He rubbed his hands together in anticipation of adventures to come.

'You mean we're going to do it again?' Kitty looked pleased. I suppose she imagined a whole summer of taking and returning, mystifying the residents of Green Hill with unexplained disappearances and reappearances.

'Not so fast,' I said. 'Just because we did it once doesn't mean—'

'I knew it,' Cam said derisively. 'You're still scared.'

'I am not. But it's silly. How many times do you think we could do it without somebody getting suspicious?'

'Oh, *Ellen*,' Kitty moaned with impatience. 'Come on and be a good sport. Make her play, Julian.'

Julian looked at me with a teasing expression. 'If Ellen's afraid . . .' He let the sentence fade away unfinished.

'I'm not afraid.'

'Don't you think your team can do it?'

I tossed my head. 'Of course we can. But it's still silly. Green Hill is too small. Sooner or later somebody would catch us, don't you see?'

'What if they do?' Cam said impulsively. 'If we return everything, what's the harm if they do find out?'

'I don't think they'd like it. Maybe Aunt Lily and Uncle Peter would understand that the weathervane was just a joke, but stealing things out of the public library—'

'It's *not* stealing,' Kitty protested, sounding like Julian had. 'We return everything.'

'I still don't think they'd like it,' I said stubbornly.

Kitty folded her arms and leaned back in the hammock with a disgruntled expression. 'We could play at least *once* more.'

Nobody said anything for a moment. Andy pulled aimlessly at a tuft of grass, watching Julian from lowered eyes.

At last, with a deliberate motion, Julian took a small spiral notebook out of his pocket.

'Once more, Ellen?' He smiled at me as only Julian could smile.

'Oh, please, Ellen.' Kitty unfolded her arms and leaned towards me, swaying the hammock.

Everyone was looking at me again. Just as they had before.

'Come on, Ellen,' Kitty pleaded. 'Be a good sport. Just one more time.'

'Oh, for Pete's sake!' I closed my eyes wearily.

'And we'll keep score this time.' Julian opened the notebook and began to write, reading aloud to us as he wrote:

'Team wins thirty points if they are the first takers.'

He paused and looked up thoughtfully. 'We ought to have a time limit of some kind.'

'Yeah,' Cam agreed. 'We ought to hide the stuff longer, make the grown-ups really wonder, make them really start looking around.'

I groaned softly and closed my eyes again.

'How's this, then,' Julian suggested. 'Each item has to be hidden by the team that takes it for two days.'

'Two days!' I opened my eyes.

'*Ell*-en,' Kitty began on me again. 'That makes it *better*. We'll have to find really *good* hiding places. It will be more of a challenge.'

'And then after the two days, the *other* team has to get it from the hiding place and return it,' Julian continued.

When there were no further protests from me, he began to write in the notebook again, reading aloud:

'Team wins thirty points if they are the first takers.

Win fifty points if what they take is not found by grown-ups in two days.

Lose fifty points if grown-ups find where it is hidden.

Win thirty points for first returners, after the two days.

Lose fifty points if anybody is caught taking or returning.'

If anybody is caught taking or returning ... How awful, I thought, to get caught ...

7 Win thirty points

That night at supper I was not very hungry. Mother had angel food cake for dessert, which is my favourite, but I didn't even finish the piece she gave me.

'No second helping, Ellen?' Father teased me. He knew how I loved angel food cake.

But I had an uncomfortable feeling, and every time my eyes met Cam's or Kitty's, we looked away from each other quickly and guiltily.

'Why are you all so quiet?' Mother wanted to know, and afterwards, in our room, Kitty said to me:

'Boy, was that ever bright, the three of us sitting there at the table like three dummies. That's the quickest way in the world for them to suspect something's up.'

When I didn't answer, she prodded me: 'When are we going to have a meeting with Andy and decide what to take?'

'Oh, I don't know,' I answered vaguely. 'What's the rush?'

'We ought to start making some plans now,' Kitty insisted. 'We want to win the points for first takers.'

'Well, we can't have a meeting tomorrow. Andy has to go to the city to the dentist, remember?'

'Oh, for Pete's sake! Why did you have to pick Andy anyway? He's so fat and clumsy, he won't be much help.'

'He got the weathervane, didn't he?' I reminded her. 'Besides, Julian's got Jenny. What help can she be?'

'At least she's not running off to the dentist when we should be having a meeting.'

I didn't really mind the delay. I wasn't in any rush to

have a meeting with Andy. And I certainly couldn't think of anything we could 'take'.

'Some captain you are.' Kitty left her parting shot and went downstairs, jerking a sweat shirt over her head.

When I came down later, she was sitting on the porch steps, no doubt contemplating the disadvantages of spending her summer with a dull sister like me.

I had only been down a few minutes when Mother came out on the porch and said Dr Drover's wife had called, inviting us all to come over for strawberry ice-cream she had made in her old-fashioned ice-cream freezer.

'Might as well do *some*thing,' Kitty said. She looked at me with an eloquent look that meant *I* never did anything. Just because I wasn't all in a stew about Andy Foster going to the dentist the next day.

Cam had gone over after supper to cut Miss Mindy's lawn. Mother had told him it was better to cut grass in the evening in extremely hot weather. So Kitty and I set out with Mother and Father to have Mrs Drover's strawberry ice-cream. Although the sun had set, it was still hot. A melancholy silence haunted the dusky twilight, and hardly a breath of air stirred. The last glimmer of dying light lay across the lake. We could see children sitting on the piers, and hear the occasional cry of a bird over the water.

'Trouble with these hot spells,' Father said as we drove along, 'is that they so often end in thunderstorms.' He scanned the sky, and Mother sighed uneasily.

'I do hate those storms,' she said.

But there did not seem to be any storm coming or any relief from the heat in any way. At the Drovers' everyone was on the side porch, where there was a very faint breeze. Very faint.

'You girls look so pretty,' Mrs Drover said to Kitty and me. 'You should always wear blue, Ellen. It brings out your eyes.'

Aunt Lily and Uncle Peter were there, too, with Julian and Jenny. After we came, all the women went out to the kitchen to get the ice-cream ready, and Jenny trailed after them. It was only a few moments before her shrill, wailing cry split the stillness.

'Good grief,' my father said.

But we thought Jenny's mother – and my mother and Mrs Drover – in the kitchen with Jenny would soon quiet her.

However, the wailing continued, in fact grew more piercing and intense.

'Better see what she's crying about,' Dr Drover said, and the rest of us all followed after him, into the house and along the hallway that led to the kitchen.

There, in the bright overhead light, stood Mrs Drover with an ice-cream spoon in her hand. Dishes had been set out along the table, and one or two already had ice-cream heaped in them. Aunt Lily was sitting in a chair holding Jenny on her lap, and my mother hovered over them, patting Jenny's shoulder and telling her she was all right.

'Well, well, little Jenny,' Dr Drover said in his deep, kindly voice. 'What's the matter with my sweetheart?'

But Jenny only buried her head deeper into her mother's shoulder and wailed louder.

'She slipped on the doorsill on her way out to the back yard,' Mother explained when she saw all the rest of us coming into the kitchen.

Dr Drover bent over Jenny and tried to see where she was hurt. Usually she liked to show everybody her skinned elbows or cut knees, or whatever had happened to her. But this time she only wriggled away every time anybody came near.

'She overtired, I think,' Aunt Lily whispered to Dr Drover. 'She's been out all day, and it's just been too much for her in this heat.'

'How about some nice strawberry ice-cream?' Mrs Drover coaxed. 'Look, Jenny, I'll fix this extra big dish for you.'

'Think *I'll* fall down,' Kitty whispered to me, as we watched Mrs Drover pile a double helping into one of the dishes on the table.

It seemed like forever, but by and by Jenny's sobs began to subside. She peeked out at us and rubbed her eyes.

Then finally she stopped crying enough for Mrs Drover to hand her the dish of ice-cream.

'Doesn't that look good, Jenny?' Father said.

'Here's a spoon,' Uncle Peter said. He took one from a row laid out on the table by the dishes and handed it to Jenny.

I thought I heard a sound in the hallway, but when I turned around, it was only Julian, lounging against the doorway. Vaguely I had the feeling that he had only now come to join us all in the kitchen to see what was wrong with Jenny.

And nothing much really seemed to be wrong with Jenny after all. She took the spoon from Uncle Peter, her sobs fading off into shudders and hiccups. She seemed quite all right now.

'Just wanted to get extra ice-cream,' Kitty said to me under her breath.

But I had a feeling Kitty was wrong. Jenny's crying had only been to attract everyone's attention. We had all rushed to the kitchen. Except Julian.

What had he done before he came to lounge by the doorway, smiling faintly at all the confusion in the kitchen?

It was the game again, I was sure. Something was going to turn up missing from the Drovers' house.

8 A problem

As soon as we got home, I hurried Kitty upstairs and told her what I thought had happened.

'You're right,' she said, with dawning understanding. 'That's why Julian chose Jenny, I bet. All along he's been thinking what a lot of fussing she could do to distract people's attention.'

She searched my face anxiously. 'What do you think Julian took?'

'Who knows? There must be a million things around that house he could have taken.'

'But he couldn't have hidden it anywhere. He didn't have time to take something out of the house and hide it anywhere. So it must have been something small. Did you notice any bulges in his pockets?'

I admitted that I hadn't even thought of that, but I had to agree with Kitty that it must have been something small. Not a book from Dr Drover's library or one of Mrs Drover's knick-knacks. And whatever it was, *we* were going to have to get it back into the Drovers' house!

Kitty sat cross-legged on her bed, frowning as she tried to guess what Julian had taken.

'I'm going to die of curiosity,' she moaned.

I began to brush my hair, and she complained impatiently, 'Ellen, how can you brush your hair now? We have to think of something for our team to take.'

'Well, I *am* thinking.'

I pulled the brush through my hair and stared at my own reflection in the mirror. What *could* we take?

'How about Mother's punch bowl?' Kitty said suddenly with enthusiasm. 'Cam and Julian might break it before they got it returned, and then our team would win.'

'And then Mother wouldn't have a punch bowl.'

'We could buy her another one.'

It all sounded so heartless to me, somehow. I felt depressed, and the brush went more and more slowly through my hair.

'Let's go to bed,' I said. 'We can talk about it tomorrow.'

'Well, can you think of anything better than the punch bowl?'

'I can't think of anything tonight.' I switched off the light. 'I'm too tired.'

But I couldn't go to sleep, and I lay awake in the dark trying to think of something my team could take. Kitty was awake, too, and kept making suggestions.

'How about Mother's ring? She takes it off every night when she does the dishes. She puts it on that ledge by the sink. We could get that easy.'

'Yes, and she'd probably have the plumber back, opening up the whole kitchen drain again looking for it.'

Kitty knew how upset Mother had been earlier that summer when the drain didn't drain, and how difficult it had been to get it fixed.

'Yeah, I guess we'd better not take that,' she admitted regretfully.

'Besides,' I added, 'think how bad she'd feel. We ought to take something that won't make anybody feel bad.'

'But it has to be important enough for the grown-ups to start searching for. We *could* take the bronze bird, I suppose, but we talked about that so much it doesn't seem any fun to take *it*.'

'Be quiet and let me think a minute. How can I think of anything if you talk all the time?'

She was quiet about thirty seconds and then she said, 'Ellen? Are you still awake?'

'How can I sleep when you talk all the time?'

I could make out her form dimly in the darkness, and I could see that she had risen in the bed, propping herself up on her arm.

'Ellen, it ought to be something that would be hard for them to return. Something so big and heavy they couldn't even move it, something like that.'

'If it was that big and heavy, we couldn't move it either, so how could we take it in the first place?'

'But wouldn't it be great if we could think of *something* that would be easy for us to take and hard for them to return?'

'I suppose so,' I agreed. 'But I can't think of anything like that.'

'I bet Julian did,' Kitty said, sinking back on to the bed with a sigh. 'He probably thought of something just like that.'

At last I closed my eyes wearily. Jenny wasn't the only one who got overtired on hot days. And Jenny didn't even have all the problems I had. She wasn't captain of any team. Lucky Jenny.

And I wondered if her little doll still lay with its face in the grass, one shoe missing, out in the dark night under the lilac bushes.

9 A surprise

The next morning Kitty and I were the last ones up, and
we decided to go swimming before eating. It was nearly
noon when we were in the kitchen making ourselves egg
sandwiches for our breakfast-lunch – and the telephone
rang.

Mother answered it. We could hear her side of the
conversation pretty well, although the phone was down
the hallway by the living-room door and we were sitting
in the kitchen.

'Is that so?' we heard her exclaim with dismay. 'Why,
I just can't believe it, something like that happening in
Green Hill.'

Whoever was on the other end of the phone spoke, and
then Mother said, 'But nothing like that has ever happened
around here before.'

Just before she hung up she said, 'I certainly am sorry.
But I'm sure you'll get it back quickly. Yes, yes – let me
know what happens.'

She came back down the hall towards the kitchen. We
could hear her shoes clicking on the floor, and then she
appeared in the doorway, smoothing her apron and shaking
her head.

'Someone has stolen Dr Drover's car,' she said. 'Imagine
something like that happening here at Green Hill.'

She had something cooking on the stove, and when her
back was to us, Kitty and I gazed at each other with
shock. But, no, it couldn't be! Julian wouldn't take a
car ...

'Julian wouldn't take a *car*!' Kitty cried wildly at me, as
soon as we could escape the kitchen and be alone on the

front porch. 'He wouldn't do that, would he?'

She searched my face. A car was a long way from a plaster bust and a weathervane.

'No, of course not, silly. He can't even drive. How could he take a car?'

'I bet he did,' Kitty insisted. She pushed back her hair, still damp from swimming. 'I bet he's been watching other people all these years and knows enough about it to drive himself.'

I tried to calm her down. 'Julian can't drive, I know he can't. He isn't even sixteen yet. You can't get a licence unless you're sixteen.'

'I bet it was Julian – oh, I just *know* it was him. What would he care if he isn't sixteen?'

'He'd care a lot, I should think. It's not legal. He might get arrested.'

'I just know it was him.'

My stomach began to feel very queer. I wished I hadn't eaten that egg sandwich. I wished I were home in the city getting ready for school to start. I wished Kitty would stop pestering me. A car – that frightened me.

'And if it's true,' Kitty went on, almost sounding like Jenny with her wailing tone, 'how can we ever return it? None of us knows *any*thing about driving!'

'Be quiet, you'll have everybody out here seeing what's wrong.'

Kitty doubled up her fists with determination. 'Now we've just got to think of something extra special – something they can never return in a million years.'

'There is no such thing,' I said unhappily. And I wanted to add that it didn't matter anyway, because we weren't going to play this game. Not me or Kitty or anybody. If Julian and Cam had taken a car – a *car* – they could jolly well have the trouble of getting it back themselves.

But they couldn't really have taken a car, I kept telling

myself in another side of my mind. They couldn't really have! It was just a wild coincidence that the car was missing when we started to play our game. Maybe somebody had driven it off by mistake – or something.

But I didn't have long to argue back and forth with myself like that. We saw Julian and Cam coming through the side hedge, along the trail that we used between Aunt Lily's house and ours.

'Here they come now – ask them, ask them,' Kitty prompted. 'Or I will, even if you are captain.'

But we didn't have to ask them anything. We watched silently as the boys came across the grass. Julian in a white polo shirt, with a leisurely, graceful walk. Cam, lanky and long-legged, a cat-that-ate-the-canary expression on his face.

'Have you heard what happened—' Kitty started to say without even waiting for me.

But before she finished, Julian held up a hand for her to stop. Glancing around from under lowered lashes, he made sure we were alone. Then he reached into his pocket and took out something.

'Present for your team, Ellen,' he said.

And into my lap he dropped a ring of keys, car keys on a metal clasp that had Dr Drover's name and address.

10 Unfair!

Before I had a chance to protest and to tell Julian we
weren't going to play, we heard footsteps coming through
the house, and a moment later Mother was in the doorway.
I didn't have time to do anything about the car keys in my
lap except put my hand over them!

'There you are, Cameron,' Mother said. 'Hello, Julian.
Cam, I told you you weren't to go out anywhere today
until you had picked up some of the things in your
room.'

'I did.'

'It doesn't look to me like they've been picked up. How
about all those clothes lying on the chair?'

'Gee, Mom, I'm going to wear them.'

Mother looked a little weary. 'Before you go out
anywhere else today, either hang up those things or put
them on and wear them. I will presume you are headed for
the North Pole. There are enough clothes there to keep an
Eskimo warm.'

With that she shook her head and disappeared into the
house again.

There was a long silence on the porch, until we were
sure Mother had gone all the way back to the kitchen.
The car keys felt as if they were burning a hole right
through my lap.

'How could you *do* that, Julian—' I started to say, but
Kitty interrupted me.

'Unfair! Unfair!' she began to chant.

Julian was sitting on the porch rail. He looked quite at
ease, very satisfied with himself and not the least disturbed
by Kitty's accusations.

'What's unfair about it?' Cam looked so triumphant I could hardly bear it.

'It is *so* unfair!' I cried.

Julian smiled pleasantly. 'We thought, as long as we're only playing one more time, we ought to take something really valuable.'

'Boy, is it ever!' Cam's eyes glistened. 'About five thou.'

And Kitty and I had been thinking about things like punch bowls. 'But what about poor Dr Drover?' I protested.

'He won't miss it for just two days,' Cam said defensively. 'His wife's got a car, he can use that.'

'You're *awful*.' Kitty bit her lower lip and glowered at Cam and Julian.

'Admit you're beaten?' Cam demanded.

I was about to say yes, we were beaten, and we weren't going to play any more anyway, but Kitty was on her feet, hands on her hips, her face close up to Cam's.

'No, never,' she said with a stamp of her foot and a toss of wet hair. 'We're not going to let you beat us. Wait and see. We've got something so – so spectacular you'll never believe it.'

A flicker of interest crossed Julian's face. 'Taken it yet?'

'Not yet.' Kitty swung around to face Julian. 'But we will soon. And then you'll see. Just wait.'

Julian smiled indulgently. He could see right through Kitty. He knew we didn't have anything planned to take. And he also knew we couldn't return that car, even if we wanted to. And I didn't want to.

'Don't you want to hear how we did it? Boy, was that ever something.' Cam was bursting to tell us how they had managed to get something like a *car*.

'Jenny's crying the other day had something to do with it, didn't it?' I asked.

My hand still lay protectingly over the car keys. But I

wanted to fire them straight at Julian's beautiful, dark-eyed face. It was his self-satisfied expression and Kitty's determination not to give in that made me hesitate. Maybe yet, somehow, there might be a way to outwit Julian. And that would be a grim satisfaction in itself.

Cam lowered his voice to a whisper.

'Dr Drover keeps extra keys in his study, in his desk drawer. And when Jenny was crying, everybody went to see what was the matter with her, and Julian slipped into the study and got the keys. How about that?'

'Oh, terrific,' Kitty said sarcastically. 'Anybody could have thought of that. And it was so obvious.' She put a lot of contempt in that last word, but it didn't worry Julian or dampen Cam's high spirits.

'Obvious or not, it worked, didn't it?'

'But how did you get the car itself?' I asked. I really couldn't figure that out – or where they could hide something so big and expensive afterwards. I was curious enough about that; afterwards I could tell Julian we weren't going to play.

'This morning Dr Drover went out to play golf with my dad,' Julian said calmly. 'They went in Dad's car. Then Mrs Drover went out in her car to shop . . .' Julian let the sentence hang.

'And Julian and I just drove it away.' Cam made motions with his hands as though he were gripping the steering wheel of a car.

'*Who* drove it away?'

'Julian,' Cam admitted. 'But I bet I could have if I wanted to.'

'I bet,' Kitty muttered under her breath.

'When did you learn to drive?' I demanded of Julian.

He lounged back more comfortably against a porch pillar and smiled at me mockingly.

'It's easy,' he said.

Which didn't answer my question but made me too vexed to ask it again.

'In broad daylight? You took it in broad *day*light?' Kitty demanded. There was a grudging admiration in her tone.

I knew that Dr Drover's house was sheltered from the house south of him by a long stretch of high hedges and trees, and there was no house on the other side. His property on the north sloped down to the road, and beyond lay another stretch of woods and then the lake. It would be easy enough for someone to drive a car out of his driveway and north along the road towards the lake, and never be seen by anybody.

'But where did you *put* it?' Kitty wanted to know next.

'That was the best part, huh, Julian?' Cam glanced over at Julian. 'Shall we tell them now, or make them wait until the two days are up?'

'Whatever you want.'

'Tell us *now*,' Kitty demanded, her voice rising.

'Stop yelling,' Cam hissed.

'All right, I stopped, now *tell* us.'

I could see that behind Julian's expression of calm an inner excitement burned, equal to Cam's eagerness and Kitty's passion. He wanted Cam to tell us, just as much as Cam wanted to tell and just as much as we wanted to know.

'It's in Miss Mindy's garage,' Cam whispered.

'In Miss Mindy's *garage*?' I blurted out.

'Good grief! Tell the whole neighbourhood.'

'In Miss Mindy's garage?' Kitty repeated in an awe-struck tone. This was only a distance of about a city block from Dr Drover's house. It was like hiding the car right under his nose. 'How did you get it in *there*?'

Cam smiled. He was getting as smug as Julian, I thought bitterly.

'Miss Mindy gave me the keys to the garage so I could

get the lawn mower while she's gone. Her car's not there now, so there was plenty of room for Dr Drover's – and nobody will ever think of looking there.'

'What if she comes back early?' Kitty suggested uneasily.

Cam hesitated and glanced at Julian. Apparently he had not thought of that possibility.

'Well, gee, why should she?' he said.

'Anyway,' Julian remarked softly, 'that's part of the risk of the game, isn't it? Maybe she *will* come back unexpectedly.'

'Boy, I hope not!' Cam began to look a little unhappy. I imagined the garage keys in his pocket were beginning to feel as much of a burden to him as the car keys in my lap felt to me.

'I don't think she will,' Julian said reassuringly. 'I'm not worried.'

Cam did not look so sure.

'You're afraid,' Julian taunted as he looked around at our dismayed faces.

'No, we're not,' Kitty blazed back at him. And to my own surprise I found myself saying, 'No, we're not!' How dare Julian think he was the only one who was daring and brave.

'Just the same—' Cam shifted uneasily and rubbed his sunburned nose.

'Relax,' Julian said to him patiently. 'The hardest part is over. And the chances are a hundred to one – a thousand to one – she'll come back early.'

'Yeah, well, I hope you're right,' Cam said. 'She's supposed to be gone another week.'

A silence fell over the porch, and then Kitty asked, 'How did you get Jenny to cry so much?'

'Fifty cents,' Julian answered.

'Big spender,' I mumbled under my breath.

Kitty shook her head doubtfully. 'But, Jenny – she's so little, she'll tell if anybody asks her any questions.'

'She can't tell what she doesn't know,' Julian said.

'Didn't you tell her why you wanted her to cry?'

Julian looked at Kitty with that long-suffering look he had. He didn't even bother to answer such a stupid question.

'And you didn't tell her about taking the car either?'

'Nope.' Julian let his gaze wander idly out across the yard and road towards the lake. Sun glistened on the water, and far out we could see two boats running close together into the wind. 'Jenny doesn't know *anything*,' he said. 'And she never will have to know anything.'

Kitty and I thought about this silently. I was glad that at least Jenny didn't know what was really going on. She was way too little to keep such awful secrets. She ought to be off with her dolls and jump ropes and Popsicles.

As we watched, a police car came along the road going in the direction of Dr Drover's house. We all watched it guiltily. Probably a policeman going to talk to the Drovers – maybe with something to report, maybe not. Maybe a policeman would come around asking us if we had seen anyone suspicious lurking in the vicinity.

And there I sat with those keys in my hand!

11 A plan

It was the police car going by that gave me the idea – and I
sat almost breathless while in an instant a whole scene of a
week or so before flashed into my mind.

'The police can drive by and keep an eye on the house,'
Miss Mindy had said.

She had stopped by our house to tell Cam not to forget
to clip the edges of the grass when he did the mowing while
she was away, and Mother had invited her in to have a
glass of iced tea.

I had been sitting on the porch reading a book, and
Mother and Miss Mindy had come out on the porch to
sit while they had their tea.

Miss Mindy was a thin, grey-haired spinster, and she
looked warm, I thought, in a high-necked long-sleeved
brown dress. Her stockings were thick and she wore heavy
old-lady shoes. A small pearl brooch was fastened
crookedly at the throat of her dress.

She didn't say much to me. She usually didn't, to
children. She regarded us all rather apprehensively when
we went by her house – as though she were sure we were
going to throw candy wrappers on her grass or pick the
hollyhocks that grew along the side of the yard. Her little
dog Sammy was usually watching us in an unfriendly
manner, too, his ears laid back and his pointed teeth
showing. If we came too close, we could hear a low growl
in his throat. For such a small dog it sounded like a pretty
mean growl. But Miss Mindy always said he wouldn't bite.

'Who's going close enough to find out?' Cam used to say.

None of us liked Sammy very much, except Andy
Foster. And Andy was the only one Sammy wouldn't

growl at. That was because Andy lived year round at the lake, like Miss Mindy, and Andy had played with Sammy when he was a puppy, before he got so unfriendly to people.

But Miss Mindy liked it that way. Sammy was her watchdog, she said, and it wasn't good to have him friendly to strangers. Strangers? We'd only been coming to Green Hill five summers now.

If we had to go into her house for any reason – Mother was always sending Miss Mindy cookies and jellies and things – we went in cautiously, and Sammy always came and growled at us.

'Now, now, Sammy, it's all right,' Miss Mindy would say to him soothingly. 'Be a good boy.' Her voice had a real affection in it when she spoke to him. It was different from the way she spoke to anybody else. She would gather him up in her arms and stroke his head so that he would stop growling. Once I even saw her bend her head down and kiss him between the ears.

So Sammy never bit any of us, but even so, we didn't like being around him, and we never stayed long at Miss Mindy's house. Jenny, particularly, was terrified of Sammy. He had chased her once when she had run across Miss Mindy's yard, and she had never forgotten it.

Miss Mindy stirred her tea, and the ice clinked against the glass.

Mother said, 'Well, I'll remind Cam about clipping the edges. He'll go down to your place once a week.'

'That will be fine.' Miss Mindy nodded. She was an orderly person and liked things done in an orderly way. Everything inside her house was always in perfect order.

'The Langs next door are going to keep Sammy for me,' Miss Mindy added. 'So everything is arranged.'

She folded her thin, veined hands on her lap.

'I hope you have a nice visit with your sister,' Mother said.

'I always do.' And it was after that that she said, 'I have notified the police of my coming absence. That's always best, you know.'

'Yes, it's a good idea,' Mother agreed.

'The police can drive by and keep an eye on the house.'

This whole scene came back to me as I watched the police car going by, and I knew what we would take! I sat a few minutes longer going over the idea in my mind to work out the details, while around me Cam and Julian and Kitty speculated about where the police would start looking for Dr Drover's car and whether or not a policeman would come around asking everybody questions.

But I hardly listened to them. I thought out the whole plan right then and there in my mind. It would work. I was sure it would work. And it was something easy for us to take and hard for them to return, just what Kitty wanted.

We might even beat Julian's team after all.

12 Meeting of the team

'*Sammy*?' Kitty exploded with surprise. 'Take *Sammy*? Ellen, you've got to be out of your mind.'

'No, it will work, really—'

'We can't even get near him,' Kitty protested.

'But Andy can, can't you, Andy?'

The three of us had gathered down by the hammock at the end of the yard to have a meeting of our team. Cam had gone up to his room to put away his wardrobe, and Julian had sauntered off with a languid wave of his hand.

'Can't you, Andy?' I repeated urgently. 'Sammy likes you. You're about the only one he likes, besides Miss Mindy.'

Andy's round, freckled face brightened under my praise. 'Yeah, I guess he likes me all right.'

'Don't you see how perfect it is?' I said to Kitty. 'Julian and Cam can't get near Sammy any better than we can, and Jenny won't be any help to them because she's so afraid of Sammy.'

'But where would we ever keep him for two *days*?' Kitty objected.

For all her enthusiasm to play the game and beat Julian's team, I thought she certainly put up a lot of arguments when somebody finally got a good idea. Besides, I was annoyed that she had hit on the one weak spot in my plan.

'That's just a detail I haven't figured out yet,' I said. 'But I thought you two might have some ideas. Just because I'm the captain of the team doesn't mean I have to do all the thinking.'

'Oh, great.' Kitty sighed with exasperation. 'You

figured out everything but the most important part.'

'I did figure out the most important part! I figured out something that would be easy for us to take and hard for them to return. That's what you wanted, wasn't it?'

This silenced Kitty for a few moments anyway.

'And it won't really hurt anybody either,' I went on. 'Miss Mindy's away, and by the time she comes home Sammy will be back again. She won't even miss him.'

'What if the Langs write to her or phone her and tell her he's been stolen?' Andy wanted to know.

'I'm betting they won't.' I was glad he had asked something I was prepared to answer. 'I was thinking, if I was taking care of somebody's pet, I would at least try a day or two to see if I could get it back before worrying them and spoiling their vacation. Wouldn't you?'

'Yeah, that's right,' Andy agreed. His blue eyes were thoughtful, and his freckles stood out dark in the sunlight.

Kitty frowned and shook her head. 'That still doesn't answer where we'd hide him for two whole days. That little monster.'

'Let me think,' I said. 'Maybe Andy could smuggle Sammy into his house somehow. He never growls at Andy.'

'I don't think I could smuggle him into my house for two days without my mother finding out.'

'Or course you couldn't,' Kitty said. 'You'd better think of something better than that, Ellen.'

'How about *you* trying to think of something?' Why did Kitty always give me so much trouble one way or another? First she was mad at me because I didn't think of something spectacular to take, and now when I had thought of something really good, she wasn't any help at all.

But then she redeemed herself. 'How about that old shed behind your yard, Andy – doesn't your mother let you sleep out in it sometimes? You could hide Sammy there and sleep out there and keep him company so he wouldn't bark or make a racket.'

Andy thought about this a minute. 'Maybe it would work,' he said at last. 'I can try.'

'Sure it would work.' Kitty's changeable temperament was on the upswing again. 'You can feed him and take care of him, and nobody will ever know he's there.'

Andy smiled hopefully.

Kitty's spirits were really on the rise now. 'Hey, Ellen,' she said exuberantly. 'It's really a great idea, really great!'

'Thanks a lot.'

13 Takers

We walked into the village and bought three cans of dog food. And a piece of clothesline, in case we had to tie Sammy up.

The heat wave persisted. Around us the grass was yellowing and dry, even the trees seemed to droop. Occasionally we saw bluejays with a flash of greyish-blue and white in the tree branches, and the sun pressed down hot against our backs as we came up the road homeward.

We agreed to meet at the shed behind Andy's yard after supper, and then go over to the Lang house together and see if we could lure Sammy away. But it was a failure. The Langs did not seem to be home. Everything was quiet. In their yard folding chairs had been set against the side of the house and a striped umbrella over a round pink table cast a solitary pool of shade below. There was no sign of anyone – or of Sammy. Either the Langs had shut him up in the house or taken him with them.

'What do we do now?' Kitty fretted.

'We'll come back first thing in the morning,' I said. 'Maybe he'll be out in the yard then.'

'I hope so.'

Next door was Miss Mindy's house – closed up, silent, with Dr Drover's car in the garage!

As we gave up on Sammy for that night and walked away, Kitty said, 'How are we ever going to get that car back to Dr Drover?'

'Maybe we could push it,' Andy suggested.

'Somebody will have to drive it,' I said matter-of-factly.

'One of *us*?' Kitty sounded sceptical but rather taken

with the idea. 'Hey, maybe I could,' she added after a moment.

'One of us will have to,' I said. 'I don't see any other way. Andy, haven't you *ever* driven?'

'Nope.'

I knew sometimes boys' fathers let them sit at the wheel a few minutes on deserted country roads where there wasn't any traffic. Our father had let Cam once. And I suppose that's how Julian knew enough to get the car away from Dr Drover's. But Andy didn't have a father. He lived alone with his mother, and he had never been allowed to try to drive, even a little. Neither had Kitty nor I.

It was a very discouraging prospect.

We went on silently and thoughtfully. We met no one along the road. It was somehow, in an eerie way, as if everybody had gone, as if Green Hill had been abandoned and left only to us, the takers and returners.

But in the morning we had better luck. Mrs Lang was out in the back yard wiping off the folding chairs and setting them up around the table. Sammy was trotting around sniffing at weeds and growling at the small white butterflies that darted over the rose bushes.

'There he is,' Kitty announced.

Andy hunkered down behind the back hedge, and Kitty and I crouched beside him, trying to see through the thick branches. It was not very comfortable. There were tiny gnats around the hedge that tickled as they touched our arms and faces, and Mrs Lang stayed in the yard a long time. But we didn't think of leaving.

Finally, Mrs Lang went into the house. The screen door closed behind her firmly, but of course we didn't know how soon she might come out again. We waited a few minutes to be sure she had not just stepped in for something and was coming right back.

'Let's *do* something,' Kitty pleaded at last. A mosquito had bitten her leg the night before, and she was scratching at the bite impatiently. 'I'm not going to sit in these bushes forever and get bitten up by bugs.'

'You two wait here,' Andy said.

We peeked through the hedge and watched as he moved around the yard until he was quite close to Sammy.

'Here, Sammy, nice doggie,' he called softly.

The grey ears pricked up. But Sammy did not move.

'Here, Sammy – come on, nice doggie.'

This time Sammy's tail began to move slowly in a lazy wag as he recognized the familiar voice. He began to walk towards the hedge.

'Hurry up, slowpoke,' Kitty whispered, in an agony because Sammy was moving so slowly.

Halfway to the hedge Sammy sat down. His mouth opened and a pink tongue hung out. He licked his lips, swallowed and sat panting from the heat. He cocked his head to one side, listening.

'This is just great,' Kitty moaned.

'Come on Sammy – nice Sammy.'

After a few moments Sammy got up again and began to walk towards the hedge.

I was nervously watching the back door of the house. I crossed my fingers that Mrs Lang wouldn't come out until we had gone – preferably not until we had been gone a long time. The sooner they missed Sammy, the worse it would be.

'I've got him,' we heard Andy whisper, and almost at once he came around the hedge again, the little grey dog in his arms.

When he saw Kitty and me, Sammy laid back his ears and began to growl low in his throat.

'You two better stay here, and I'll go on ahead to the shed,' Andy said. 'We don't want him growling and barking at you and have Mrs Lang out here.'

So Kitty and I stayed where we were, and Andy loped off along the back road towards his house.

'I'm being eaten alive here,' Kitty complained, swatting at the pesky gnats.

'Well, so am I.'

She made no reply to this, but sat back on her heels and scratched her mosquito bite and swatted at the gnats.

When we left at last, Mrs Lang had still not come back out of her house.

Just as well, I thought. Maybe she wouldn't miss Sammy for hours and hours yet.

We met Andy by his shed, and he agreed to hang around the shed during the day to keep Sammy from being lonely and barking. If he barked, someone might hear. I thought Andy had the hardest part, because it would be awfully dull hanging around that shed all that hot day.

But he had the dog food and a pan he had sneaked out of the house to put water in. And he had made a bed for Sammy out of an old cardboard carton lined with rags.

'I'm all set,' he said rather cheerfully.

He was so eager to be helpful, always so eager to please and be part of our crowd. I was glad I had chosen him first. It was the first time anybody ever had. It seemed to have made up to him for all the times the other boys had laughed at him for being slow and fat, and for all the times we had let him just hang around us without caring one way or another whether he was there or not. He was sure a big help now.

As Kitty and I started home from Andy's, walking along the Lake Road on the edges of the grass, carrying our shoes and feeling the prickles of the dry blades against our toes, Dr Drover came along, driving his wife's car.

'Hello gypsies,' he called to us when he saw our bare feet.

'Hi.'

We stood in the grass, squinting our eyes because the sun was blinding on the glass and chrome of the car.

'How about a nice cool ride home?' he said to us.

Kitty and I looked at each other guiltily. Of all people to offer us a ride, poor Dr Drover – whose car was gone. I felt Kitty nudge my arm gently. We couldn't stand there gaping at him forever.

'Sure, that'll be swell,' Kitty said. 'Won't it, Ellen?'

'Sure,' I agreed hastily. I even tried to smile. How deceitful I was getting. I climbed into Dr Drover's wife's car just as though nothing were wrong.

'I hear your car got stolen,' Kitty said innocently as she settled back against the seat.

How bold she was! I cringed inwardly.

'That's right,' Dr Drover answered with a wry smile. 'But it will turn up before long, I expect.' His eyes had little lines around them that deepened when he smiled.

'Are the police looking hard for it?' Kitty wanted to know next.

I wished she would just be quiet and let us have our ride home and get out of the car.

Dr Drover laughed. 'They're looking, but I don't know how hard.' He laughed again, as though somehow he could not picture anybody working too hard at anything in peaceful Green Hill. Even the police.

'Have they got any clues?'

'None that I know of yet. But it will turn up.'

'I sure hope they find it for you soon,' Kitty said. She couldn't have sounded more sincerely concerned.

'Great performance,' I said to her, as we walked up to our house and Dr Drover's car disappeared down the road.

'I may grow up and go on the stage someday,' Kitty answered airily. She swished up the stairs, held the door for me with a sweeping bow, and entered dramatically into the house.

She might be on the stage someday, I thought, but I doubted if she would ever grow up.

14 A triumph

Kitty and I had our moment of triumph when we walked over to Julian's house. He and Cam were in their bathing suits, just setting off for a swim in the lake, and I like to think we took some of the pleasure out of it for them.

'Here,' I said without any introductory remarks.

I thrust Sammy's collar at Julian. His surprised expression was worth crouching in those gnat-ridden old bushes. I felt Kitty nudging me happily.

Cam stared down at the collar in Julian's hands. 'Good grief, what's that?'

Julian recovered himself almost immediately. But he didn't look too happy. 'It's a dog collar,' he said to Cam. 'Can't you see that?'

'Yeah, I can see that. What dog collar?'

Julian and Cam looked at Kitty and me curiously.

'Sammy's,' I replied coolly.

It was indeed a moment of victory. Maybe they had got the extra thirty points for being first takers, but we had sure given them something to worry about now.

'*Sammy's* collar!' Cam's startled reaction was all we could have hoped for.

'Very clever,' Julian admitted. His dark eyes narrowed, and he studied Kitty and me intently.

'When the two days are up, we'll tell you where to find him,' I said.

'Hey – we told you where the car was,' Cam protested.

But I only smiled calmly. 'That's because you wanted to tell us. There isn't any rule that we have to tell. Julian didn't make any rule like that.'

Cam looked at Julian to come up with a good answer

for this, but Julian only shrugged. 'No, I didn't make any rule about that.'

Cam was still mad. 'Why the big secret?'

'Never mind. In two days we'll tell you. You may have a long way to go, so be prepared.'

With that I clutched Kitty's hand and pulled her after me with as much nonchalance as you can manage when you walk away pulling somebody after you.

'What did you say that for?' Kitty wanted to know as soon as we were out of earshot.

'I want them to worry,' I said. 'I want them to think maybe we've put Sammy in a crate and shipped him to the moon.'

'Hey—' Kitty's eyes lighted up. 'That's a great idea, Ellen.'

'Anyway, they'll have something to worry about for the next two days.'

'They sure will.' There was admiration for my tactics in her voice. Good old Kitty.

When we left Julian and Cam, we walked out of our way to go past the Lang house, but there did not seem to be any commotion there, no police car in sight investigating the report of a stolen dog. So far so good. I wondered how poor Andy was doing in that hot shed with that mean little dog.

All the rest of the day Kitty and I waited to hear if the Langs had missed Sammy. But they weren't as good friends of our parents as the Drovers were, so they could miss Sammy without calling to tell Mother about it.

Late in the afternoon Kitty and I volunteered to drive to the store with Mother, rather to her surprise. We thought we might learn something about driving if we watched Mother closely. I sat in the front seat beside her and Kitty sat in the back, hanging over the front seat to watch everything Mother did as she drove.

But it didn't seem to do much good. I guess you can't learn to drive in ten minutes of sitting beside somebody who isn't even explaining what she's doing. There was a lever on the steering column, and every once in a while Mother pushed it. When she had to back out of a parking space, she twisted around to look over her shoulder – and met Kitty's face.

'For heaven's sake, Kitty, sit back. I can't see a thing.'

I knew the accelerator from the brake, and where the ignition key went, but that was about all. And maybe Dr Drover's car wouldn't work the same. Ours was what Father called an 'automatic transmission'. What if Dr Drover's wasn't? Then there was a lot more to the driving. I knew that much.

Kitty and I were pretty discouraged – and besides not learning anything, we ended up helping bring the groceries in and getting them put away.

'This is some fun,' Kitty muttered to me as she unloaded canned goods on the kitchen table.

When I went upstairs, I found Miss Mindy's garage key lying on my dresser with a scribbled note from Cam:

'Your move.'

15 Time limit

The next morning, Friday, at ten-thirty, the two days'
waiting to see if the grown-ups and the police could find
Dr Drover's car was up.

Julian called me on the telephone to tell me.

'You can take the car back any time now.'

His voice came coolly to me over the phone. How
satisfied he must have felt to have outwitted everyone, I
thought.

Mother was about three feet away dusting a what-not
stand in the hall. 'I know,' I said to Julian. It was all I
could say with Mother so close.

'I just wanted to wish you luck.'

'You're so kind.'

I glanced at Mother. She seemed very busy dusting, but
you never could tell about mothers.

'Good luck,' Julian said.

I hung up without answering. Good luck yourself, I
thought, picturing Julian and Cam struggling with the
growling Sammy.

But then I thought about Dr Drover's car, and my heart
sank.

By eleven o'clock Kitty and I were over at Andy's shed.

He was sitting on an old chair with Sammy lying across
his knees. We could see he had fed Sammy some of the dog
food and put water in the pan he had brought out of his
house.

Sammy never failed. He laid back his ears and began to
growl before Kitty and I were even through the door.

'Ssshh, Sammy,' Andy said soothingly. He put his face

down close to the little grey head and smoothed his hand along Sammy's back. 'That's a good boy, ssshh.'

The growling grew softer and finally stopped, although Sammy continued to watch us with a distrustful stare.

'Did you ask your mother about sleeping out here last night?' I asked Andy.

'She said she didn't know why I wanted to but it would be all right.' Andy smiled. He was feeling lately everything he touched turned to success.

Kitty plunked herself down on the floor with a deep sigh.

'How are you on driving?'

Andy shook his head and grinned sheepishly.

'That's what I thought.'

'Kitty and I drove to the store with Mother, but we didn't learn much,' I explained to Andy. 'Do you suppose Dr Drover's car is an automatic transmission?'

'I don't know,' Andy said. He fondled Sammy between the ears, and Sammy's tail began to wag slowly. His tongue lolled out again, and he began to look less ferocious. He wasn't really a bad-looking little dog, I thought. His hair was short and curly, and he had a cute tail. If only he weren't so unfriendly.

'The best thing for us to do,' I began thoughtfully, 'is just wait another day or two, and try to get in a car with somebody every chance we get. Every little thing we can learn will help.'

'But the two days are up,' Kitty said promptly.

'Julian didn't make any rule about *having* to return the things exactly when the two days are up. He just said we had to hide them two days to see if anybody could find them. Okay. Nobody found the car. Good for Julian's team. Now we'll return it when we're good and ready.'

Andy and Kitty thought about this silently.

'Yeah,' Kitty said at last, 'I suppose a couple more days might help us – but what about winning the thirty points for being first returners?'

I had forgotten that.

'Let me think,' I said, in what I hoped was a confident tone of voice. 'Now we took Sammy Thursday morning, so they can't take him back until Saturday morning, tomorrow.'

'And that's probably just when they'll do it,' Andy put in.

'Maybe not – maybe they'll wait.'

'Why would they wait, silly?'

Why indeed? Kitty was right. Once the two-day time limit was up, they would want to return Sammy as fast as they could to get the thirty points.

'We're going to lose any way you look at it,' Kitty said glumly.

'But what if they can't return Sammy?' I reminded her. 'He might snap and growl and run away from them.'

Kitty's face brightened momentarily. 'Wouldn't that be great!' Then she sobered. 'You know Julian. He'll think of something. I don't think we should wait, I think we ought to go and get that car right now.'

'In broad daylight?'

'Well, then, as soon as it's dark.'

'What do you say, Andy?' I looked over at him uncertainly.

'Whatever you say.'

He was certainly agreeable.

'Will you try to drive it?'

'I'll try.'

16 Delay

But our plans to meet that night at seven-thirty and wait for dark were ruined. The heat wave was ending, and by seven o'clock a high wind had sprung up. The sky grew darker and darker. The wind tossed the trees frantically, and all the boats were off the lake. Thunder rumbled nearby, and flashes of lightning streaked the late sky.

'I hate these storms,' Mother kept saying.

One year some power lines had come down, and we had been without electricity for a day. A lot of damage was done to houses and trees, too, and ever since that time Mother always fretted when thunder began.

Kitty and I watched from the window in our bedroom. There was no hope of going out that night.

At eight the storm broke in full fury. Lightning bolted down through the dark sky, and the trees bent in the wild wind. We had to run around and help close windows and bring things off the porch. The lights dimmed once but stayed on – to Mother's immense relief. She hadn't thought it was nearly as much fun as we had, the time the electricity was off, and we had to use candles to get ready for bed.

'I bet Andy's mother won't let him sleep in the shed tonight, and Sammy will howl his head off,' Kitty decided.

'Nobody will hear him over this storm.' I tried to sound encouraging, but Kitty was not much cheered up.

Another problem was created by Cam's arrival at our bedroom door. 'Didn't get the old buggy back yet, huh?' he gloated.

'None of your business,' Kitty snapped.

'There's no rule says when we have to return it, just so

the two days are over,' I told him. I tried to make it sound as though we had some secret, wonderful reason for waiting.

'You'll never get it back.'

'We will *so*,' Kitty said.

'How?' He lounged in our doorway, arms crossed, a smirking expression on his face. 'Who's going to drive?'

'That's our affair,' I said, kicking Kitty, who had opened her mouth to say Andy.

'Yeah,' Kitty said. 'That's our affair. We'll probably have better luck than you'll have with Sammy.'

'We're prepared.'

'I hope you get bitten to pieces,' Kitty said.

Cam just smirked again and started to move on to his own room. Then over his shoulder he added:

'I wouldn't wait too long if I were you, about the car. You know those car batteries run down if the cars aren't driven for a while.'

'What do you mean?' I said, startled. What was this now about batteries? 'Cam, come back here—'

He returned and leaned against the door frame again, enjoying my distress.

'What about the batteries?'

He shrugged. 'They run down, that's all.'

'Then what?' I asked impatiently. I didn't even know cars had batteries. I thought those were just in radios and flashlights.

'Then they don't start.'

'They don't *start*?' Kitty cried.

'It's very sad.' Cam made a long face. 'They just don't start.'

'Why didn't you tell us about these old batteries before?' I demanded.

'It's not "these old batteries". It's just one.'

'Well, one. Why didn't you tell us before?'

74

'You never asked.'

I glared back at Cam.

'How long before it runs down?' Kitty asked.

Cam shrugged. 'It depends. Old batteries run down faster. Dr Drover's might still be good, it's only been a couple of days. But you better not wait too long.'

With that he left, and I didn't bother calling him back. With the storm outside, we didn't have any choice but to wait. And it would probably be a long wait, until dark came again the next day ...

Kitty seemed to read my thoughts, for she returned to the window and stared out at the rain, 'By tomorrow that old battery's going to be dead, I just know it.'

'Why can't you ever look on the bright side of things?' I cried. 'Dr Drover probably has an extra good battery in his car. Doctors have to be able to rely on their cars. They keep everything just right.'

But a loud crash of thunder drowned Kitty's answer – and I wasn't sure I wanted to hear it anyway if she couldn't at least try to look on the bright side of things. There must be a bright side somewhere – but it was even getting difficult for me to find it ...

17 A chance to win

The next day seemed endless. The storm had blown down small branches, which lay scattered across the lawns, but otherwise there had not been any serious damage anyplace at Green Hill. And the air was cooled by the storm. The day remained overcast and cheerless, and I almost thought I'd rather have the hot sunny days that had passed, stifling and scorching as they had been.

Overnight the grass had seemed to turn green again. But a wind persisted, ruffling the lake, and nobody went out to swim or to take out boats.

There wasn't anything to do.

It was about noon when Julian came over, Jenny tagging along behind him. We got Cam and then we walked along the road a way, so we could talk without being overheard.

'Better put sweaters on, girls,' Mother had called as we started out, and Kitty bolted upstairs to get the sweaters, so we could get out without further interruption.

'Okay,' Julian said, when we were a safe distance from the house. 'The two days are up. Where's Sammy?'

He would go now and get Sammy and take him back – and we still had no hope of returning the car until nightfall, even if we could manage to do it at all. But there wasn't anything I could do but tell him where Sammy was.

'He's in that shed behind Andy's house.'

'That's sure a long, long way,' Cam said sarcastically.

Jenny had trailed along after us, and I glanced over my shoulder at her. But she couldn't hear us.

'You won't get much help from Jenny, you know,' I said. 'She's scared of Sammy.'

'I think the rest of the team can manage it,' Julian said.

We stood a few moments more sort of looking at each other, and then Kitty and I started back to the house.

'Lots of luck,' I said.

'Same to you,' Julian answered. Then he said, 'You go on home, Jenny.'

'No.'

'I think it's going to rain some more. You'd better get home.'

'No.'

Kitty and I watched with satisfaction. If Julian couldn't get rid of Jenny, he couldn't go to get Sammy.

'No,' Jenny kept saying.

At last Julian gave up and started on with Cam, Jenny close behind.

'Ha, ha,' Kitty said to me jubilantly.

But her jubilance didn't last long. We had not quite gotten back to our house when Jenny appeared again, running after us.

'What are you doing here?' I asked her – somewhat rudely, I'm afraid.

'Cam said your mama's making a cake, and I can lick the frosting bowl.'

'Mother's making a cake?' I asked Kitty.

She shrugged elaborately. 'How should I know?'

It had been a mean trick for Cam to pull. We went in the house, and Mother was not baking a cake at all. She was sitting at the dining table with Aunt Lily, drinking a cup of coffee.

'I want to lick the frosting bowl,' Jenny complained.

'But, darling, there isn't any frosting bowl,' her mother said sweetly.

'I want to lick the frosting bowl. Cam said there was cake and I could.'

'Cam was teasing you,' Mother said. To Aunt Lily she added. 'These boys. I just don't know what gets into them sometimes.'

'But I want to lick the frosting bowl.'

Then, to my great surprise, Aunt Lily – who never scolded Jenny – sighed with exasperation and said, 'Jenny, be quiet. I am sick and tired of your whining.'

Even Kitty gulped with surprise to hear that.

I didn't learn what happened until afterwards – that Sammy had gotten away from Cam and Julian and run off into the woods.

All I knew was that about the middle of the afternoon, Cam came back home, looking rumpled and dirty, and went up to his room and slammed the door.

'What's wrong with him?' Mother asked, lifting her head from her sewing.

Kitty and I had spread out the Monopoly set on the dining-room table for want of anything better to do. We were dying to rush upstairs after Cam and find out what was wrong, if he would tell us. But we stayed at the Monopoly board as long as we could stand it.

About ten minutes later Kitty said with assumed nonchalance, 'I'm tired of this game. I'm going upstairs.'

'Put the board away, girls,' Mother reminded us from the living room. 'I'll be setting the table for supper soon.'

Mother always planned things so far ahead. It was only about three o'clock, and we never ate till six.

Kitty and I piled the paper money and property cards into the box every which way and shoved it into the bottom of the sideboard. Then, casually and slowly, we went upstairs.

Cam wouldn't answer our knock at first. 'Go away,' he said.

'Something's happened,' Kitty whispered, her eyes glowing. 'Something went wrong.'

'Cam,' I begged. 'Open the door.'

At last he came to the door and opened it about an eighth of an inch.

'Go away,' he said again.

'What happened?' Kitty got her toe into the opening. 'Did you return Sammy?'

'We'll let you know when we return him,' Cam said. He had washed his face and changed his shirt.

'You *didn't* return him yet,' I said.

'Go away,' Cam said again, and managed to push Kitty's toe back outside and get the door closed.

Kitty stuck out her tongue at the closed door, but then she turned to me excitedly. 'They didn't do it yet, Ellen. Maybe we can still win.'

'Let's make sure,' I said. 'Maybe it's just a trick.'

'How can we make sure?'

'We can walk by the Lang house and see if Sammy's there. Or we can go to Andy's, and maybe he'll know. That might even be better.'

'Don't forget your sweaters, girls,' Mother called again as we started out. 'It's quite cool today.'

But this time we already had our sweaters, and we hurried off before she could think of something for us to do – like get that table set for dinner.

At Andy's house we learned nothing. He said he had gone in to eat lunch, and when he went back to the shed afterwards, Sammy was gone. He hadn't seen anything of Julian and Cam.

'Why weren't you watching?' Kitty fussed.

'I had to eat some lunch, didn't I? You want me to starve?'

'Missing one meal wouldn't hurt you any,' Kitty said, which wasn't kind, considering how fat Andy was.

'Listen, Andy's done more than his share already,' I said to Kitty. 'Taking Sammy and keeping him quiet for two days.'

Kitty still looked mad.

'I guess we'll just have to go by the Langs' and see,' I said.

Andy went with us, and the three of us walked along the Lake road more and more slowly as we approached the Lang house. There was no sign of Sammy in the yard, front or back. I was wishing we knew the Langs better and could just run in and say hello, casually, and see if Sammy was inside.

And then Mrs Lang, who had been sitting on the porch, saw us and came to the steps and called to us:

'Children – children – would you come here a moment, please?'

'Oh golly,' Andy said under his breath.

I guess he thought we'd been caught for sure now.

Lagging, we went up the walk to Mrs Lang's front steps. She was a small, plump woman with greying hair she kept dyed red. A lot of magazines lay on the porch table, and she had been drinking a glass of lemonade or iced tea or something. She had probably been pretty once, I thought, but that red hair sure looked strange on her.

'You children haven't seen Miss Mindy's dog around anyplace, have you?' she asked. Her forehead was wrinkled with a frown of concern.

'Miss Mindy's dog?' Kitty echoed innocently.

'Yes, you know – that little grey dog, Sammy. Miss Mindy's away and we've been taking care of him, and he's run off somewhere. Nobody's seen him, and I'm getting so worried.'

'Have you told Miss Mindy?' I couldn't resist. I felt it would be doubly awful if Miss Mindy were worried, too, on the visit to her sister that she had told Mother was always so pleasant.

'No, I haven't called her,' Mrs Lang said. 'I didn't want to worry her unnecessarily. I thought the dog would be back by now. Once before he ran away, and he came back the next day. But that was when he was hardly more than a puppy, and I never dreamed such a thing would happen again.'

Then she added, 'I finally notified the police after he'd been gone the first night.'

I felt goosebumps on my arms when she said that.

'If we see him, we'll let you know,' I forced myself to say. My voice sounded shaky to me, but Mrs Lang didn't seem to notice.

'I'd appreciate it very much,' she said. 'Sammy's never done this before, except that one time. I feel responsible, you know, taking care of him for Miss Mindy.'

'I bet you do,' Kitty said. Her actress blood was stirred again, and she gazed up at Mrs Lang consolingly. 'But he'll probably be back soon. Try not to worry.'

'Thank you, dear,' Mrs Lang said, 'but it's hard not to. You let me know if you see him, and you might ask the other children around here to keep an eye open for Sammy too.'

'We will,' Kitty promised solemnly.

So even though we didn't know until later that Sammy had gotten away into the woods, we did know that he hadn't been returned yet.

'We still have a chance to win,' Kitty gloated, as we moved off down the road.

And then she began to run ahead of us, making swooping motions like a bird.

Andy walked us home and then went down to the lake to watch the waves made by the high wind.

I followed 'swooping bird' up the steps to the porch.

We still had a chance to win, all right – but we still had that car to drive to do it.

18 Returners

The rest of the afternoon seemed longer than the whole rest of the week put together. The hands on the clocks stopped.

We were going to meet Andy at seven.

By five o'clock Kitty was so excited and flushed looking that Mother said she wondered if she was coming down with something. She almost got sent to bed.

We didn't miss Cam until supper time. We thought he was still up in his room being mad, but when it was time to eat, Mother didn't call him to come down.

'Where's Cam?' I asked.

'He said he was invited to Julian's for dinner,' Mother replied.

'When did he go?'

I thought Mother might be suspicious of my interest in Cam's dinner, but she was busy passing salad plates.

'A while ago. While you were out.'

Kitty and I exchanged glances across the table. Whatever Cam and Julian were up to, we were willing to bet they weren't sitting calmly around the dinner table at Aunt Lily's house. (Later, of course, we found out they had returned to the woods to search some more for Sammy.)

Supper dragged on. During dessert Father began talking about Dr Drover's car and how it was the first time he could ever remember a car being stolen from anyone at Green Hill.

'I thought sure the police would have located it by now,' he said.

I thought Julian and Cam would have burst to hear that. How clever they must feel, proving they were smarter than the police.

'That car may be a long way from here by now,' Mother said.

Kitty choked on whatever she was eating, and Mother said, 'Heavens, Kitty, drink some water.'

I thought the meal would never end.

After supper Kitty and I did the dishes, with one eye on the clock. Just before seven Mother came out into the kitchen and said she was going to drive into the village with Father and asked if we wanted to come.

'No, I guess not, thanks,' I said. I even yawned elaborately to make it look as if I were too tired to go.

'Me neither,' Kitty said.

Mother looked at her a moment, to assure herself that Kitty didn't really need to be in bed.

'All right, then,' she said. 'We won't be long.'

We waited until the car was out of sight, and then we set off along the back road and the edge of the woods, for Andy's house.

Usually it was about a quarter to nine before full darkness came, but because the day had been so overcast, it was dark before eight-thirty.

The door to Miss Mindy's garage creaked when we opened it, and we stopped and waited. But nothing happened. Andy had brought a flashlight, and we went in cautiously.

There was Dr Drover's car.

'Battery's probably dead,' Kitty prophesied before we even got the door opened.

'Be quiet and try to help,' I said.

'I couldn't get the key into the door lock, and finally I gave up and let Andy try.

When the car door opened, we all stood there looking in uncertainty, the smell of car interior strong in our nostrils.

'You might as well get in by the wheel,' I said to Andy. We had opened the door on the passenger side, so he slid across the seat and got behind the steering wheel.

I got in next, and Kitty started to scramble after me, when Andy said, 'Somebody ought to stay outside and let me know what's happening.'

'What do you mean, what's happening?' I said.

'I've got to back up first. I've got to know how close I am to the sides of the garage door.'

Back up! I hadn't even thought of that.

'Oh, Andy, do you think you can back it up?'

'There isn't any other way to get out,' he said, which was pretty obvious.

'See if it even starts,' Kitty hissed, her head ducked down to talk to us as she stood outside the car.

I held the flashlight, and Andy found the ignition switch and got the key in.

He turned the key.

There was a funny grinding sound, and Andy turned off the key in panic.

'Try again,' I whispered.

'That battery's dead,' Kitty said. 'I knew it, I just knew it.'

'Be quiet a minute,' I begged her.

The last thing I wanted was for Andy to get nervous – and Kitty could make a Sphinx squirm.

Andy turned the key again, but nothing happened except that grinding sound.

Then I remembered that I had seen Mother press down on the accelerator with her foot when she turned the ignition key in our car.

'Push down on the accelerator a little when you turn the key,' I said.

'Where's the accelerator?'

'Oh, great!' I heard Kitty sigh to herself.

It was too dark in the car to see anything, and I aimed the flashlight down by Andy's feet.

'It's that one on the right. The other's the brake.'

'Oh, yeah.' Andy sounded more assured now that he could see something.

'This is never going to work,' Kitty said through the doorway.

'Be *quiet*,' I snapped at her. 'Do *you* want to get in here and try?'

'I could do better than you two.'

Andy put his foot on the pedal and turned the key. The car made a sort of racking noise, but nothing much else happened.

'Try again,' I encouraged Andy. 'Hold your foot down longer.'

And for once Kitty was quiet, inspired no doubt by the car's making some kind of a sound.

Andy put his foot on the pedal and turned the key.

And miraculously, the engine sputtered and caught. The car was started.

'Are you going to turn on the lights?' Kitty asked.

We hadn't thought of this before. It would be easier to get out of Miss Mindy's garage unnoticed by somebody at the Lang house next door if we didn't have the lights on. But on the other hand, we couldn't see what we were doing very well without them.

'I guess we better risk using the lights,' I said.

'Where are they?'

'Oh, Andy – don't you even know where the lights are?'

'They're somewhere around here. There ought to be a knob or something.'

He started poking at knobs while I held up the flashlight. The windscreen wipers started first – and then the radio.

That really scared us, for it came on with a blare.

By the time Andy got the radio off and the windscreen wipers stopped, Kitty was jumping up and down with desperation.

'What are you two *doing* in there?' she kept saying.

Finally we found the lights – but they seemed so dazzling, lighting up the whole garage and alleyway behind, that Andy switched them off in a panic.

'I think we ought to try without the lights first,' he said. 'Gee, everybody can see us with them on.'

'We'll have to use them on the road, but maybe we can get out of this garage and away from the Lang house without them,' I said. 'After that it won't matter so much if we're seen.'

And then Kitty, as she always managed to do somehow, redeemed herself.

'That thing on the steering wheel tells whether you can go backwards. I think it's called "reverse",' she said. She got into the car and leaned across me to show Andy the lever she meant on the steering column. Above it was a dial with the letters P R N D L.

I didn't know what the other letters meant, but it seemed like R would be a good guess for 'reverse'.

Andy pushed the lever, and a red indicator moved from P to R on the dial.

'Now get out, Kitty,' I said, 'and let us know if we're too close to the sides of the doors.'

'Don't squash me,' she cautioned.

'Don't stand close.' When Kitty was out, I closed the door after her. 'All right, Andy, go real slow now.'

'I wasn't exactly planning to go racing out,' he answered. There was nervous tremor in his voice. Poor Andy, I thought. Poor Ellen, too.

Slowly and fitfully the car crept back.

I opened the door a little again, so I could hear Kitty's directions.

'The other side – the other way—' she began saying almost at once.

Andy turned the wheel and pressed on the accelerator again timidly.

Inch by inch the car jerked out of the garage. Fortunately the doors were very wide, and there was almost no danger of hitting the sides. Kitty stood well out of the way, holding the flashlight against the side of the car so she could see where it was going.

We didn't try to turn as we went out, like I had seen Father do when he backed out of our garage. We just backed straight out, until we had the car standing outside of the garage.

'Close the garage doors, Kitty,' I called softly.

'I have to do all the hard work,' she complained. But she hurried to them quickly enough. And when I got a glimpse of her face in the light from the flashlight, I could see the exuberant expression and the glow of daring in her eyes.

'Now let me in.' She came to the car, and I moved over closer to Andy to make room for her.

Just as she started to close the door a light went on on the Langs' back porch, and we heard Mrs Lang call:

'Sammy ... here, Sammy ...'

Her voice had a discouraged sound, as if calling Sammy from the back door were something she'd been doing before without any luck. I thought of her standing there, searching the darkness beyond the porch light, hoping the little grey dog would come running towards her across the yard.

After a few minutes the porch light went off. There was silence.

But a feeling of unhappiness overwhelmed me, and I wanted to get out of that car and run away somewhere.

Even Andy and Kitty seemed subdued.

But after a few seconds Kitty said, 'She's gone now. Let's get started.'

The car was still in reverse, and Kitty held the flashlight so that its beam fell on the dial. P R N D L.

'We want to go forward now,' she said.

But there certainly wasn't any F on the dial.

'Try that next thing,' I whispered to Andy, and he clicked the arrow to N.

But when he stepped on the accelerator, nothing happened.

'That's not it,' Kitty said unnecessarily. 'Try the next one.'

Andy moved the arrow to D. This time, when he put his foot cautiously on the pedal, the car jerked forward.

'Don't drive back in the garage!' Kitty cried out.

The car jolted and stopped.

'I think I have to back up some more before I can turn,' Andy said. His voice was hoarse with strain.

Kitty and I waited, holding our breath, while Andy put the car into reverse again, jerked back a few more feet, and then returned the arrow to D.

This time, as the car started to move forward, he turned the wheel, and we began to swing around. There wasn't much clearance between the garage and the car as it turned, but there was enough. At last we were headed in the right direction, and we began a slow, lurching drive along the back road beside Miss Mindy's back yard.

The clouds had parted, and a pale moonlight showed the outline of Miss Mindy's fence. My heart was in my throat, and I was sure any moment people would come running out to see what was going on.

The back road didn't run through to the Drover house, unfortunately.

'We'll have to turn up here and go around Miss Mindy's house and get on the Lake Road,' I said.

'How about the lights now?' Andy asked.

'Let's go a little farther without them, as long as we can see something,' Kitty said.

I looked over at Andy now and then, his round face bent forward as though he could drive better if he got closer up over the wheel. I felt as if I couldn't swallow, and my heart was pounding. Oh, I would be glad when this was *over*.

'We've got to remember to wipe our fingerprints off the door handles and the steering wheel,' Kitty announced. But my mouth felt too dry to try to answer her.

We inched around the side of Miss Mindy's yard, and the Lake Road lay ahead, a pale line before the trees in the moonlight.

'Shall I turn the lights on now?' Andy wanted to know.

'They're so bright,' Kitty objected. 'Everybody will see us.'

'It won't matter when we get on the Lake Road,' I managed to say. 'If anybody sees us, they'll just think we're another car driving by.'

'At two miles an hour?'

This was somewhat of an exaggeration, but we *were* going pretty slowly. Kitty was right. To anybody sitting on a front porch, a car creeping by slower than they could walk would look mighty odd.

'Can't you go a little faster, Andy?'

'I'll try when I get on the Lake Road.'

The car hunched past the hedges at the side of Miss Mindy's yard.

'Turn the lights on now,' I said, as we started to turn on to the Lake Road. 'And speed up a little.'

Andy found the right knob for the lights on his first try this time, switched them on, stepped harder on the accelerator, and turned on to the Lake Road. And as we made the turn, coming suddenly from behind the row of hedges, our headlights blazed full into the faces of Cam and Julian – startled and blinking in the sudden brightness.

From a large box Cam was holding a dark figure sprang out and ran in front of us. It was Sammy!

'*Stop – stop!*' I screamed to Andy.

There was a piercing yelping sound, and the road swayed crookedly in front of us as Andy stepped on the accelerator in his panic instead of the brake, tried to swerve, and crashed the side fender of the car into a tree.

Kitty was thrown against the door, which she had not closed securely, and it flew open. She fell out on the grass – and Andy's arm hit the horn. Above the sound of the dog's sudden squeal, the car hitting the tree, Kitty's cry, and the horn blowing, I heard someone screaming, '*Stop – stop!*' It was a moment or two before I realized that it was I screaming.

Lights blazed on at the Lang house. First porch lights and then yard lights. And with those lights and the headlights of the car, aimed crookedly across the road towards the house, all was plainly in view for the Langs to see as they came running towards us: the boys in the roadway with their empty box – the stolen car crashed against the tree – Kitty stumbling to her feet crying—

What they could not see at first was Sammy, for the front wheel of the car had gone over him, and he lay under the car in the darkness of its shadow.

19 Losers

Father said we were all equally to blame.

Mother said it was all Julian's fault because he had started the game; he was the ringleader, and we had just followed him.

Like sheep, I thought miserably.

I will never forget the sight of Sammy lying in the road under the car that night. He didn't seem fierce now, and no growl started in his throat when Mr Lang picked up the lifeless body tenderly in his arms. Mrs Lang was crying, and Kitty was crying, and I was crying. There were tears blurring Andy's blue eyes, too. Andy had only wanted to do what we did and be part of our crowd. And Sammy had only wanted to get home again, across the road to Miss Mindy's house.

Aunt Lily and Uncle Peter cut their summer short and returned to the city. We didn't see Julian and Jenny again before they left, but I found Jenny's doll one day where she had left it that afternoon in the shadows under the lilac bushes. It was still lying face down in the grass, as though to shut out from its gaze all the unhappiness around it.

Dr Drover and Mrs Drover did not say much. Mrs Drover had always been kind to us, and her face was so sad when I saw her it made me feel worse than if she had started to scold. I heard Dr Drover say to Father:

'Their own feelings are punishment enough without my starting in on them about taking the car.'

We had to pay, all of us kids, for the damage to the car. But there was no amount of money that would bring Sammy back.

The worst part was when Miss Mindy came home. She came home to an empty house that must have been haunted by memories of a little grey dog, paws clicking across the kitchen linoleum, tail wagging as he stood with front feet braced up against the screen door . . . Once I had seen her bend her head down to kiss him between the ears.

We had to go over, of course, and try to explain what had happened and tell her we were sorry. We had decided we would offer to get her another dog.

She did not invite us in, and we stood awkward and helpless by her door. Her lips trembled as she tried not to cry, but tears welled up in her eyes and trickled down her cheeks as we told her it was just a game and we hadn't meant to hurt anybody.

'We're really sorry, Miss Mindy,' I said miserably.

Kitty's usually perky face drooped with sadness. 'Maybe we could get you another dog.'

'No . . . no.' We could hardly make out Miss Mindy's words.

Cam couldn't hide his disappointment. 'Are you sure?'

And that was when it really struck home to me, the incurability of what we had done. For in a kind of flash, I realized that we had wanted to replace Sammy for *our* sake, so we could tell ourselves that we had mended the wrong we had done. But to Miss Mindy, there was no replacing the little animal she had loved – and we had destroyed. Chilled and silent, we all grew up in that moment.

We had to leave her with tears on her cheeks, and the walk out of her yard to the road seemed unending as we felt her watching after us from the door.

When we were away from the house, Cam said bleakly, 'I don't know why she doesn't want another dog.'

But he *did* know why. We all knew. And after that we

didn't talk any more. We walked all the way home in silence along the dusty summer road.

We could never go by her house after that without feeling the sadness and lonesomeness we knew were there, in the yellow house behind the trees and the rose bushes and the neatly kept lawn. We knew that Miss Mindy was in there, old and prim and all alone.

We were all losers.

Carol Beach York
The Witch Lady Mystery 60p

Young Oliver had put up his services as a raker of leaves to auction.
The highest bid had come from old Mrs Prichard and so it was the
leaves in her garden he had to rake.

But Oliver was putting the job off. It was just too scary . . . because
Mrs Prichard was the Witch Lady, living alone with one black cat in
a ghostly house of closed up rooms . . .

Dead Man's Cat – a mystery 60p

Mr Morley was dead and somewhere there lay hidden his fortune of
thousands. Michael and his sister Queenie watched as the strange
Mrs Poldini entered the dark tenement to call old Morley's secrets
from the grave.

They'd soon learn many strange things – not least about the
dead man's mysterious stamp collection and his elusive, knowing
yellow cat who held more secrets than even Mrs Poldini could
reveal . . .

Judy Blume
Then Again, Maybe I Won't 70p

Tony is thirteen and he's just moved house. Now he lives in the
best part of Long Island, surrounded by luxury homes and swimming
pools. Next door there's Joel who's a dab hand at shoplifting.
Joel's older sister Lisa gets undressed every night with the lights on
and the curtains open. Tony's mother thinks everything's swell
on Long Island. She wants Tony to be just like the kids next door –
or does she ?

It's Not the End of the World 70p

Karen is twelve and her world is crumbling. First of all her mother
and father were arguing all the time – then her father moved out
and didn't come back. Now he's going to Las Vegas to fix up a
divorce. Karen's new friend Val has been through it too . . . But
maybe Karen and her brother Jeff and baby sister Amy can somehow
stop it happening – or maybe they just don't stand a chance.

Kevin Crossley-Holland
Sea Stranger, Fire-Brother and
Earth Father 60p

Three stories of Wulf the Saxon boy and Cedd the holy man who
converts him to Christianity in the dark and dangerous years of
the seventh century: Wulf, lying dreaming among the ruins of the
Roman fort, becomes Cedd's first convert after his sea-journey from
Northumbria to the land of the East Saxons; Wulf's new life of
peace and learning among the monks is envied by his own
brother Oswald — then someone sets fire to the crops the monks
have been growing ... Wulf makes the dangerous journey to see
his old friend when news comes that Cedd is dying of the plague.

Nina Beachcroft
Under the Enchanter 60p

The Hearsts are an ordinary Yorkshire family who rent an
ordinary Yorkshire farmhouse for their holiday. But soon Laura
and her brother Andrew discover something very out of the
ordinary ... above the stables there lives an elderly man — the
malevolent and smiling Mr Strange. Laura is wary, but Andrew likes
him. Then Andrew begins to change, drifting into a weird
dreamworld ...